30

LANDER'S KINGDOM

Tim Hara was a man with a mission: to apprehend the notorious outlaw Dane Lander, and to solve the mystery of the strange woman kept captive in the outlaw's fortress. Tim's background was supposedly that of a thief whose love of gold would gain him entry into Lander's lair. But nothing went as smoothly as it should have done. Only his lightning quick brain and guns could offer him any hope of survival — but would they be enough?

TOM HARPER

LANDER'S KINGDOM

Complete and Unabridged

LINFORD
Leicester

First hardcover edition published in
Great Britain in 2002 by
Robert Hale Limited, London

Originally published in paperback as
'Lander's Kingdom' by Wes Yancey

First Linford Edition
published 2003
by arrangement with
Robert Hale Limited, London

British Library CIP Data

Harper, Tom, *1914* –
 Lander's Kingdom.—Large print ed.—
 Linford western library
 1. Western stories
 2. Large type books
 I. Title II. Yancey, Wes
 813.5'4 [F]

ISBN 1–8439–5056–1

Published by
F. A. Thorpe (Publishing)
Anstey, Leicestershire

Set by Words & Graphics Ltd.
Anstey, Leicestershire
Printed and bound in Great Britain by
T. J. International Ltd., Padstow, Cornwall

This book is printed on acid-free paper

1

On The Run

Tim Hara smiled at his secret thoughts as he raced his willing horse over the shale, his sun-darkened face almost flat against the animal's dusty mane, the odour of hot animal flesh mingling with his own body sweat. They were heading at a dangerous pace towards the dried-up creek.

Tim smiled thinly as he thought about the wisdom of this exploit. Would it work? Was he crazy to attempt it? Maybe he was riding into more grief than glory . . .

Another mile went past and then he eased to a slow canter and patted the panting horse, wondering if he'd been noticed. He sure hoped so after this display! Maybe the hidden spies of the hardcases, perched on a rocky hilltop and armed with a telescope glass had seen him.

He brought the horse down to a walk, got out the makings and rolled a cigarette that he lit with a thick sulphur match. Nostriling smoke, he pushed back his stained stetson and ran a hand around his neck, under the wet yellow bandanna.

Yeah . . . maybe he'd been noticed . . . then the scheming could start . . . and maybe one Tim Hara would end up dead!

He glanced back to the distant ridge over which he'd come at such hell-bent speed. He could visualize the posse pounding along the old trail, heading towards Famoso, that stinking, ramshackle outlaw town. Well, the posse and Sheriff Dugald could take care of themselves . . .

As for himself, he was only human and he had doubts. A man could die quickly out here. He had a good horse, two Colt .45s and years of experience in this kind of country. But maybe a man could tempt Fate once too often. Now, if the spies who were probably watching felt trigger-happy and indisposed to listen to him, the whole thing could burn up before it even got started.

He smoked slowly, rolling with the horse, his eyes fastened on a distant rocky outcrop. It was a spine of limestone, whitish-pink and broken, haloed by the hot sky.

Tim Hara had the kind of eyesight that could pick out details at incredibly long range. He took off his thin buckskin gloves and stuffed them into a saddle-bag, then he rubbed his hands down his black flannel shirt. He was ready to handle his Colts.

He'd seen something move in that outcrop.

After some minutes of riding he nudged the roan into the gully. Hoofs crushed wild plants, fresh with a yellow bloom, and some cholla cactus. Then a lithe figure went running towards a pony standing patiently farther along the gully.

Tim Hara leaped from his saddle,

sprinted after the running figure and threw his arms around the man, bringing him down.

Tim's arms pressed against soft mounds. Surprised, he stared into an oval of a tanned face. Under the jacket was a light blue shirt — and two significant bulges. With a smothered oath, Tim whipped off the 'man's' grey hat — and stared at a mass of curled blonde hair.

'What in heck are you doing out here in these badlands?' he demanded, annoyed at his initial mistake.

'Minding my own business!' she rapped back. 'Let me go, you dirty owlhooter!'

'Your business? And what the devil's that?'

'What's it to you? Take your hands off me.' Her fierce blue eyes challenged him. 'I saw you a long way off.' Her gaze fell to the twin Colts. 'Another drifter from Famoso, I reckon.'

He jerked to his feet. 'Why were you watching me?'

4

'Forget it.'

'Where are you from? You don't live in Famoso. There are only three women in that helltown and you ain't one of them.'

'Maybe you'd like to know my age and where I was born?'

A grin lit his face. 'Well, you should have a name.'

'I'm Janet Lander. Maybe that means something to you? It should — if you're fresh out of Famoso.'

He wasn't easily startled, but her surname caused him to narrow his eyes momentarily. Lander! Dane Lander was the man he had to kill or capture!

Cautiously he said, 'I've heard of a man called Dane Lander. Most of the rannigans in Famoso know about him but few seem to know where to find him right now.'

'That's my father.' She pushed past him. 'I'm going. I'm not talkin' any longer. You're probably some no-good galoot on the run . . . '

He laughed, revealing strong white

teeth. 'That's good, comin' from the daughter of an outlaw. Yep, I know about Dane Lander — heard talk about him in the saloon in Famoso. You could do me a good turn, Miss.'

'I'm the daughter of a wanted man, as you said,' she retorted. 'And I don't do good turns for strangers.'

'It isn't much. Just take me along to where I can have a chinwag with your pa. I'd like to join up with a hard man like that. I want a job that — '

'You could poke cattle,' she snapped.

'I'd rather have easy dinero. From what I hear, your pa is the kind of boss I like . . . '

'Then you're a fool!' She reached for the leathers dangling from her pony's bridle. 'And I was right the first time — you're no good!'

'Hold it,' he said. 'I really want to meet Dane Lander. Don't ride out.'

But she had forked her mount and the pony jumped forward, brushing past him. Another jab with her heels and the animal was taking her swiftly away from the outcrop. He vaulted into the saddle and thrust his bigger horse in pursuit. She sent her pony around a screen of chaparral and prickly-pear, where greyish leathery lobes branched out in eerie patterns. His big roan got into stride and he was almost level with her when another rider cantered around the thicket. The girl's cry of greeting rang out.

'John — there you are! Tell this hellion to leave me alone!'

The three riders swirled their mounts around, taking stock of each other. Tim Hara saw anger mounting into a handsome young face. The man jigged his big black mare close to Tim's roan.

'Have you been botherin' Miss Lander?'

'He has!' the girl whipped back.

'I just asked her a simple question,' began Tim Hara. 'I wanted to know if I could meet Dane Lander.'

The young man's face twisted. 'Only an owlhoot would want to meet him — or the law — and you ain't no

7

badgetoter. You've got drifter written all over you!'

'Watch your tongue,' Tim advised. 'Who the hell are you anyway?'

'He's John Hertzog,' the girl said. 'His father is a big rancher over in — '

'You don't have to explain to this ranny,' cut in the young man. 'He's going — pronto!' And with that remark he closed with Tim Hara, grabbed a leg and tried to tumble him out of the saddle.

Tim grinned faintly. John Hertzog was impulsive and not nearly experienced enough in rough-house. Tim's two hands scooped under the other's armpits and at the same time his knees dug into the roan. The horse backed steadily under the direction — and John Hertzog was snicked clear of his saddle. He fell to the dusty ground with a thud, then jumped up like a mountain cat and rushed at Tim Hara.

It wasn't Tim's idea to get tangled in a useless argument. He had more important tasks to accomplish and fighting a red-faced young galoot in front of a girl wasn't one of them. But there wasn't much alternative. John Hertzog came in angrily and tried to unseat him from the roan.

He partially succeeded. Tim was forced to slide his boots to the hot, dusty ground and face the enraged rancher's son.

'Now look, amigo — I got no fight with you,' began Tim. 'I don't care who you are or what kind of relationship you got with this girl. I just wanted to know where I could find Dane Lander, and seeing she's his daughter — '

'You — you tried to make a fool outa me — in front of Janet!' shouted the other. 'You damn Famoso scum, I'll show you!'

Tim sighed and screwed up his eyes as the other came rushing in, fists flailing. John Hertzog carried a single gun in a holster that seemed new. He didn't attempt to drop the gunbelt; his anger was too immediate for such niceties.

Gloved fists flashed towards Tim's face, and he jerked into reactions born of many such brawls. He ducked and his stained hat fell to the ground. Then his own fists rammed out, into the gap through the other's bunched hands and at the angry face.

Tim Hara placed his quick one-two right and the young fellow staggered back under the impact. Again drawing on the harsh lessons he had learned, Tim waded in while John Hertzog was trying to get his balance. Another couple of hard fists landed on the young man's chin as his swinging arms cut into air. John went back, trying to dig into the arid ground. But a long left snapped back his head and he sat down violently.

When he looked up, Tim Hara was staring down at him without any pleasure. John Hertzog then made another mistake. With a cry of humiliation he went to draw his gun. Everything was wrong. He was at a bad angle, his holster was stiff and new

— and he was slow.

He found himself staring into the bores of two Colts. They had appeared in the hands of the dusty, sweaty drifter as if by magic. He could have sworn he didn't see them leave leather.

'Don't be a blasted fool,' Tim grated. 'Simmer down, feller. You've got everything tangled to allfire hell!' Tim flicked a glance at the speechless girl. 'I beg your pardon, Miss. I'm just trail-happy. I think I'll blow.'

For a small girl she had a big temper. She blazed. 'You'd better — before I scratch out your eyes!'

'Yeah . . . ' Tim Hara gave a faint smile. 'Maybe I'll see you again, Janet. After all, I still figure to meet up with your pa — and then maybe I'll understand why you're out here in the badlands.'

John Hertzog got slowly to his feet, dusted his pants and then gently fingered his right eye. It was already swelling.

'You're a mighty curious cuss,' he

said. 'If you're gonna blow, do us a favour and hightail it now! I came here to see Janet, not to brawl with a — a — '

'A no-good,' Tim finished for him. He holstered one gun and reached out for the dangling reins of his horse.

'Yep! Well, courtin' is better than fightin'! Wish I had time for it. But I still hanker to meet up with Dane Lander. Now there's a man! But finding him is provin' to be mighty difficult. I did hear he has some sort of natural fort up in the Yellow Hills. Nice and handy to Palermo and the banks and stages. Not forgettin' Sansemo is only forty miles away, at the head of the railroad . . . And then there's Famoso — a fine town if you want to buy some guntoters. Yeah, this part of the Texas-New Mexico border is plenty interesting. Well, I guess I'll just ride along . . . '

The girl had been staring at the horizon. Now she swung back to Tim Hara. 'If you weren't so busy yapping, you'd have noticed the trail dust. It's probably my father, looking for me. Maybe you'll soon get your wish, trail man — but maybe you won't like it!'

2

The Big Man

The town of Famoso was accustomed to the sudden arrival of hard-riding horsemen, but usually they were hellions in a big rush to get somewhere safe. The five riders who entered the huddle of shanties, tents and adobe-walled hovels came with a pounding of challenging hoofs and halted in a swirl of alkali dust outside the largest building. This was the saloon which, in deference to the many vaqueros who used the place, bore the legend: CANTINA.

Sheriff Luke Dugald glared around, then slid from his shiny saddle, hitched his cord pants up around his ample waist and hooked a thumb near his single, low-slung Navy Colt 45. He entered the saloon, ramming the batwings, placing heavy boots down on dirty bare boards as if exterminating crawling things with each footstep. He saw the upraised glances of the motley collection of men who were sitting at tables and standing indolently at the pine bar counter, and he shouted the first belligerent words that hit his mind.

'Anybody seen that cuss with the black shirt and twin Colts? Big feller — leaner than an Injun lance — rides a nervy big roan.'

Nearly all turned insolently to their card games and glasses of tequila and bottles of Michigan whisky. Only one answered — which was good enough for Luke Dugald's purposes. He was the bartender.

'Well, he ain't here as you can see, Sheriff!' Then: 'Say, what brings you from Palermo? You know this ain't a healthy place for the law.'

'I asked a question!' Luke bawled. He glared around. Maybe a lot of his antagonism was a bluff but all the same he felt a bit mean. The hell-for-leather ride hadn't been exactly fun — not with a brassy sun broiling down.

'Any jigger see that rider enter this two-cent town? He came this way, a mighty tricky sidewinder by the name of Tim Hara. Here's a wanted poster. Maybe you can stick it up somewhere. You — bartender — tack it up behind your counter where the no-account rannigans that infest this place can see it!'

Two more of the posse had entered the cantina and one said: 'There ain't a roan in the street, Luke.'

'I asked some men but they hadn't seen him ride in,' said the other.

The bartender was staring doubtfully at the wanted poster and the crude picture of Tim Hara. A poor reproduction it might be, but it was good enough for identification.

'Seems like this galoot tricked us,' growled Luke Dugald. 'Hell — all this ride for nothin'.'

'Guess he branched off somewhere,' said a posseman. 'A clever gent — and what a horse!'

'What did this buckaroo do, nick your loose change?' sneered a bearded man sitting at a table.

He got a laugh from the customers in the saloon, but it also gave Luke Dugald a cue.

'He raided the assayer's office and got away with four bags of gold.' The sheriff glared around, pushing his hat back, an indignant expression on his moustached face. 'Just think of that — four bags! All pure nuggets — no damned dust or ore!'

A small, white-haired man, hunched at a table like a gnome, hatless and wearing a black frock-coat, spoke up in a gentle, courteous voice. 'How did he get the stuff, Sheriff? Surely the gold was in a safe?'

'He busted the safe.'

'How?'

'Dynamite — what else? Knew how to do it, too. Wadded the lock with clay and used blankets to muffle the sound. No one heard a damn thing . . . '

'How then did you get on his trail?'

'Wal, he gave himself away. We got to askin' questions in town and he made a run for it. He had a horse all saddled up — gold and everything it would seem. We rode damned fast after him, then we lost him. But I figure he came this way.'

'I think maybe you're wrong,' said the little man with a smile. 'You know as well as I do, Sheriff, that there ain't no more than thirty men in this town — never is. A newcomer gets spotted right away.'

The possemen, getting restless, exchanged disgruntled looks with the sheriff. He knew he had played out the charade as far as it could go. But he had one last word. He looked sarcastically at the small, white-haired man he knew as Lawyer Baily.

'If I don't get this rannigan, Tim Hara, I hope the badlands drive him loco.' He knew that Baily was a confidant of Dane Lander and of any outlaw who needed advice, and he was sure the information about his pursuit of Tim Hara would soon get to the all-powerful owlhoot leader. 'That gold will be the death of him,' Dugald said.

'Let's get out of here,' said one posseman. The other nodded.

Sheriff Dugald smiled. He had led the men on this chase knowing they would go only so far. They had only so much patience. He was the lawman, the hired gun, the one who took responsibilities — and blame.

Tim Hara was one heck of a man, Dugald thought. There could be nothing but admiration for an individual who would take on a hardcase like Dane Lander — to say nothing of his men and the desert, the gold and the heat.

The wanted poster he had left with the bartender was genuine. Tim Hara was known from Pecos to San Antonio as an outlaw wanted for robbery and murder. He was a real hard *hombre*, not easily understood when his history was known, and perhaps the victim of many myths.

Sheriff Luke Dugald stamped out of the cantina, threw a ferocious glance at an idling Mexican and hit his saddle.

'Let's git, men. The whole thing's a dead duck.'

Two possemen came from across the road where they had been investigating a horse corral. They were unshaven, lean-faced and angry. They were cronies of Sheriff Dugald. He figured they wouldn't be friendly any longer if they knew the truth behind their long ride.

'Seems damn like it!' grunted one man. He threw Dugald a glance. 'You said he'd head for this rat town, Luke . . . '

'Well, I figured — '

'I reckon he cut across the badlands. I said that an hour ago — but you wouldn't listen.'

'I thought sure he was aimin' for Famoso.'

'A jigger with any sense carrying four bags o' gold would steer clear of that bunch.' said the man curtly.

The sheriff drew in a deep breath. He

realized his judgment was being questioned and he had to come up with good answers. 'And what's for a man out in the desert? Seventy miles of hot shale and dust until you git to Skaggs. And Skaggs ain't much at all when you get there.'

'It's near the Mexican border, a good place for a man with stolen gold.'

The sheriff wiped his brow and felt fed up. He couldn't tell the possemen the truth, that he had orders from men in authority representing the commanding officer at Fort Worth, General Charlton. His orders had been decided on at a meeting attended by himself, Tim Hara, Captain Morgan of the U.S. Cavalry, and a federal town marshal from Sansemo.

One thing he knew for certain: Tim Hara wasn't heading for the border. Even the tidy sum of money in gold wouldn't tempt that man . . .

'We'd better ride back,' he said harshly. 'You men have work to do, I'll allow, and I can't tackle the badlands alone.'

They rode slowly out of the lawless little town, watched by speculative eyes. One interested watcher was Lawyer Baily, a hunched little man, white-maned like a preacher and gentle-voiced — but as nasty as poison in a well.

★   ★   ★

Far from Famoso, among the chaparral, the Joshua trees, the yellow-bloomed cholla cactus and the white, sun-bleached rocks, one of the biggest men Tim Hara had ever seen stood by his jet-black horse and surveyed the girl, John Hertzog and Tim Hara with a sort of calm amusement. For Tim Hara there was no need for introductions. This big, powerful man clad in an ornate, hand-stitched silk shirt and fine black serge pants, was Dane Lander. He was about fifty years of age and weighed some two hundred fat-trimmed pounds. He had crisp, curled grey hair and a face that was almost Indian in its hawk-like lines. His pale blue eyes indicated Scandinavian ancestry; in fact Dane Lander had once been as blond as the corn in summer.

He sat in the saddle with authority that approached majesty. His single gun lay in a polished brown holster that had been hand-worked by an Indian craftsman. A new Winchester with a gleaming, varnished butt lay in his saddle holster, near a coil of rope and a water canteen. This was the man who ran Lander's Kingdom, the man with a record price on his head.

'So you ran off, Janet.' His voice was gently patient, as if he were talking to a child. 'To meet some young man, eh? Well, I guess that's natural — but dangerous, too.'

'I met John at that party six weeks ago . . . ' She flushed.

'Yep, I remember that dance. I gave you permission to go because I realize the hideout is a bit restricting to a young girl . . . '

'Oh, Dad — I like being with you, but — but — '

'I know, my dear — the place is kind of grim for a young girl.' He nodded slightly. 'The time has come, I think, for you to leave. You can go to your aunt in Abilene. It's been on my mind for some time.'

His fatherly voice, full of concern and as well-modulated as that of any Southern gentleman, was astonishingly deceptive — and Tim Hara was well aware of it. He'd been thoroughly briefed on this renegade; he knew how many men he had killed and he had memorized a list of his various other crimes. A long list.

John Hertzog rushed in. 'If you don't mind my saying so, I figure Janet ought to live in town — among civilized people — not gunslingers, thieves and — and — '

'Did you ask my permission to see my daughter?' Lander asked. The change of tone was like a back-handed slap in the face.

'Well, no, sir! How could I?'

Dane Lander sniffed disdainfully and

fixed his stare on Tim Hara. His eyes were cold, calculating. 'Who are you?'

The four Lander riders jigged their restless horses around the outlaw leader and glared at Tim Hara. They were wary men. Their clothes were travel-stained, dirty, practical. Two wore rawhide chaps over their pants. One had a Mexican steeple-shaped hat. Their boots were dusty, worn, witness to the fact that out of the saddle they walked rough ground. One man owned two guns in cutaway holsters, a fact that Tim Hara quickly noted. The other three had real working guns, and each man had a rifle, stashed snugly in saddle leather. There was little about these hardcases to show they had robbed countless thousands from banks, freight lines, stages and gold miners — but maybe their cut was just that of highly-paid gunslingers. Maybe the real loot was cached away and only Dane Lander knew where.

'I'm nobody,' Tim Hara said. 'Just a feller, ridin' through — '

'You were seen heading towards Famoso with a posse after you,' was the dry rejoinder. 'Then you veered over the badlands.'

'Now, how the heck — '

'I have men posted for miles around — and we have our means of communication.'

'Heliograph.' Tim nodded, watching.

'Exactly. But we didn't ride out to see you. I wondered where Janet had gotten to. However — ' Dane Lander gestured to one of his men. 'Take a look in those saddle-bags, Ralph. Our friend won't mind.'

'Say, I ain't letting you poke around in — ' But Tim cut himself short as a gun appeared in Dane Lander's hand.

Tim Hara allowed his mouth to twist into a snarl as the blank-eyed man called Ralph worked his mount closer. He stayed silent but mean-looking as the man slipped the straps on the saddle-bags and ran dirty brown hands inside.

'He's a drifter, Dad,' the girl said. 'I

26

watched him ride up while I was waiting for John. And he asked about you.'

'Did he now?'

'Said he wanted to join up with you.'

'Mighty interesting.' The pale blue eyes went to Tim once more, thoughtfully but revealing nothing as they swept over the twin Colts, the trail dirt, the nervy horse that looked as if it could leap over a ranchhouse.

'Gold!' cried the man called Ralph. He held up one of the small bags of nuggets.

It was always a magical word, Tim Hara reflected. The men around Dane Lander nudged their horses closer, interest stamped in their faces. Even John Hertzog furrowed his brow and shot another glance at Tim.

Dane Lander's gun steadied. 'Where'd you get that gold?'

'I picked it up.'

'Did you work for it?'

'Nope.'

'Search more, Ralph.'

'There ain't no need,' said Tim lazily. 'I got four bags like that.'

'And you wanted to work for me?' The questioning voice was cool, deadly.

'I wanted somewhere to hide out,' Tim said. 'I could pay for my keep and I could work — if there's anything interesting to do that needs fast guns.'

'We can always use fast *guns*,' Dane Lander said.

'Fine.'

'I take half of any loot we pick up and the other half is shared among my men. This ruling will also apply to your gold.'

Tim Hara leaned forward on the pommel. 'I worked for that gold! It's mine!'

The big outlaw leader jerked a nod at Ralph. 'Get the gold out of those saddle-bags.' He shot a glance at Tim. 'I sure hope your guns are faster than your brain, *hombre*! We take the gold whether you join us or not. There are no rights in Lander's Kingdom except the privileges I give you. You work and you obey orders.'

'You mean to tell me all I get is a share of half that gold?'

'That and your life.' Dane Lander's scrutiny was both confident and curious. 'We could shoot you right now. Did you really think you could enjoy the safety of Lander's Kingdom and keep that gold?'

'I figured I could make a deal.'

'You can — and I just told you what it is.'

Tim Hara appeared to fume, then he nodded slowly, grudgingly. 'It's a deal.'

The big man grinned. 'Congratulations. You just saved your life.'

3

Desert Gunshots

The Yellow Hills rose out of the badlands like ugly teeth. The hills were surrounded by forty miles of shale and alkali where only the rattlers and cactus thrived. There were waterholes — but Dane Lander had them carefully hidden. Without water the law was easily discouraged.

Tim Hara knew all about the Yellow Hills — on paper. He had spent some hours poring over maps of the area. The hills could not be disguised or made invisible. Desert wanderers knew about them and had poked into them for as long as the white man had been around these parts. The desert lands, encroaching nearer to the green of Palermo with every decade, guarded the Yellow Hills like a moat around a castle. And the yellow rocks, rising in a tangle of gullies and small box canyons to a series of peaks that stretched for four miles and were the backbone of the rocky fastness, formed a kind of fort — the home of Lander's Kingdom.

An army couldn't venture into these unknown hills without risking the life of every man, if the purpose was to engage in combat with Lander. But one man might penetrate the Kingdom . . . and learn some of its secrets.

Tim Hara rode along with the big outlaw's gunslicks. The gold had been taken from him and John Hertzog had been sent packing miles back — after Janet had promised to meet him again. At this, Lander had maintained a set face during Janet's goodbye to Hertzog; not displeased, but thoughtful. This, Tim Hara thought, was one problem for the outlaw that couldn't possibly be solved with guns.

'You don't say much,' sneered the blank-faced rannigan called Ralph. He rode close to Tim, hunched, holding the leathers in one gloved hand, the other hanging limp as if he were resting his arm. 'You ain't regrettin' hitching up with the boss, are you? Seemed to me you weren't too happy with his proposition.'

'That was a mistake,' Tim said mildly.

'Well, maybe Mr Lander will take kindly to you. Me, I figure you acted kind of dumb, haulin' all that gold right into our laps. You didn't tell us how come you laid hands on it.'

'It was in a safe in the assayer's office in Palermo. I cracked it.'

'Yeah? What's your name? Don't tell me it's Smith! We get more wanderers with the name of Smith than I figure is natural.'

'Tim Hara. I guess you could say I'm known around San Antone.'

'San Antone? Ain't my kind of town. I'm from north — Denver City, only I ain't hankerin' to go back.'

That would figure, Tim thought. Probably a hanging party would welcome the sight of this renegade. But to

Tim he was just an underling. The real target was Dane Lander. A quick slug would kill him, but at the moment that would amount to suicide. And there were Lander's secrets. Dane Lander had to talk, reveal things, give up his secrets — all this before he gave up living.

The man had had luck, creating a fort out in the wilderness and defying the law while amassing riches. He had kept his authority among a bunch of owlhoots who normally cared little for human life and property. He ruled and imposed conditions that wouldn't be accepted elsewhere. From all accounts he dealt out swift retribution to any man crazy enough to go against his will.

The pileup of yellow rock came into sharper relief with every mile travelled. The crags, haunts of eagle and buzzard, showed their distinctive features in the glare of the sun. The party of riders jogged on slowly — until a flurry of gunshots cracked in the distance.

Lander reined up and the others followed suit.

As far as the eye could see there was no movement of man or beast, but there were two long gullies just ahead, stretching for about half a mile each.

Again the shots peppered the air. 'Six-shooters,' said Tim Hara to nobody in particular. Then, boldly, because he had to get on the inside track with Dane Lander and a humble role was no use, he said: 'You got men out here, Lander?'

'No.' The blue eyes were like ice. 'You can call me Mister, if you please!'

'Sure.' Tim leaned on his saddlehorn. 'Sounds like somebody's firin' back.'

It was obvious that rifles were answering the six-shooter, each shot coming to the ear with a flat crack.

'Two rifles,' said Tim. He wanted to make himself known, and being a loudmouth was one of the best ways. He was there to stir something up and he figured he'd start right now. 'And they ain't Winchesters. Seem like older shooters to me.'

'We got ears!' one man rasped.

'Let our gold-robber show how smart he is,' said Dane Lander. 'We might find out something about him.' He turned his jet-black horse slightly and moved him off. 'What else, friend?'

The whole party rode with the leader, but the walking pace didn't increase. The owlhoots weren't too interested in other folks trying to kill each other.

'Two old rifles and a Colt, I figure,' said Tim Hara. 'And the ruckus is comin' from that gully.' He pointed. 'You tell me the rest . . . '

'Indians,' said Dane Lander coldly. 'They favour the rifle but few of them around here have Winchesters as yet.'

'That's what I thought,' Tim said.

Janet Lander turned in her saddle, breaking the silence she'd maintained from the moment they had set off for the Yellow Hills. 'Dad, can't you take a look? Someone might be in trouble.'

'We never shed any tears over Indians.'

'But you could take a look.'

'My dear, I poke into nothing that doesn't concern Lander's Kingdom or doesn't show a profit.'

'How can you be so hard?'

'We have had this kind of argument before — '

'We certainly have! About everything! Lawlessness — killing — hiding — everything!'

'You're challenging me again . . . '

'I just think you should ride over to that gully,' she cried. 'Someone needs help. If — if you won't do it, I shall!'

And with that she jabbed at her pony. Within seconds she had her pony in a gallop, heading for the unknowns attacking each other in the sunken slot of arid land.

'Come back, Janet!' Dane Lander ordered.

Obeying the impulse to make himself prominent, Tim Hara raced his animal after the girl. Their horses soon brought them to the first decline into the cactus- and boulder-filled cut in the earth. They reined up. Instantly a number of things were clear. Two Indians were crouched behind boulders. The third person was tall, wearing a new stetson and showing fair sideburns.

'It's John!' Janet cried.

'He oughta be miles away from here,' Tim said. 'What's his game?' He slid from his mount and went to the girl. 'Ride off and take cover. I'll take care of this.' He pulled his rifle from his saddle holster. 'Git — before your father gits annoyed.'

She heeled her horse away from the edge of the gully and, as more shots sounded in the still air, he slid forward, hugging the earth and bringing his rifle up.

It was going to be tough on the two Indians but they were, in actual fact, trying to kill. Possibly they figured a lone rider was worth robbing. That's all the setup could be. From his knowledge of these areas, he thought the Indians were Mescalero Apaches who came down from the Sacramento Mountains on sporadic raids. Usually they rode in small packs of eight or nine braves. Two lone Indians was a bit unusual, but — He quit thinking about it and triggered.

The weapon barked and one of the Indians jerked and then pitched to the side and lay in an ungainly heap. Tim Hara sighted as the second Indian twisted around. He fired. A head shot. It was all over.

'It's all right,' Tim called. 'I got both of 'em.'

John Hertzog moved from behind a boulder as the other riders cantered up, reined and stared down at the scene. Janet slid from the saddle and came down the side of the gully.

'John, I thought you'd gone home . . .

'I — I just thought I'd ride back and — and — well, have another talk with your father,' stammered the young fellow.

'Then you're a fool!' came Dane Lander's angry voice. Tall in the saddle of the big black, he glared down at John

Hertzog. 'I told you to get going!'

'And I wanted to say that I won't let Janet be kept in that damned outlaw roost!' Hertzog shouted back.

'You'd be wise to hold your tongue. A pity the Indians didn't finish you.'

Janet flashed an indignant look at her father. 'You are becoming impossible,' she cried out. 'You have no humanity! This way of living — beyond the law — is colouring your whole personality!'

Dane Lander's deadly anger mounted. There was one thing he couldn't face and that was loss of authority. Rebellion could be put down with guns, but this display of antagonism from his own daughter was something he hardly knew how to handle. But he had to do something about it. He didn't dare show weakness.

He rode his horse down the gully slope, then he nudged the animal close to John Hertzog, crowding him against a large boulder. He drew his Colt.

'I'm telling you to vamoose! To leave Janet alone. I'll decide on who her friends will be. Now git!'

His show of power was put over with all the authority a big man on a big horse can command. It looked good. Tim Hara, watching keenly, decided that here was a weakness in the outlaw leader that he might exploit: Dane Lander had set his own daughter against himself!

His thoughts were cut off as Janet Lander cried out in protest. 'You will not choose my friends! I like John and I'll see him again.'

Lander's eyes became glittering slits. 'Get on your pony. We're riding back to the hills.'

Lander jigged his horse forward. The animal rammed into John Hertzog and sent him stumbling among the rocks. He fell and lay there, momentarily stunned.

Lander stared down at him, a hard expression settling into the hawk-like lines of his face.

Watching, Tim Hara knew what was in the man's mind. Something in his expression warned of the next action. Tim couldn't explain these hunches he often got — but many times his acute sixth sense had paid off.

In the few seconds that were left in which to act, Tim nudged his roan down into the gully. The horse moved steadily, muscles rippling, nervy but under his control.

Janet couldn't get to Hertzog because her father's big black was in the way. The young man stirred and Lander pulled back on the reins. Tim saw the horse's head move to the left, nostrils flaring, hoofs pawing at shale. Hertzog was still on the ground and the hoofs of the big black were striking only inches from his head.

Tim Hara made his roan spring at the last second, knowing full well the outlaw's intention. His horse shouldered between the black and the young rancher. The black had to jig backwards as the roan used its weight.

The natural instinct of any horse was to pick a way over anything that even resembled an obstacle, but if the rider made the animal tread repeatedly on the same patch of ground the hoofs would fall heavily and without regard.

John Hertzog, conscious now, scrambled away from the horses. Janet Lander paled, staring at her father. He, in turn, glared into Tim Hara's eyes.

'You interfering swine — I'll bring you to account for this!'

'I had to do something,' Tim said, almost casually. 'Half-a-ton of horse-flesh can't do a man much good. I don't think your daughter would like that.'

Suppressed anger showed in every line of the big outlaw's face. 'You'll taste my discipline, *amigo*!'

'Well, I guess you're the boss,' Tim drawled.

'Get going!' Lander snapped. 'We're wasting energy riding around in this damned heat!'

'And what about John?' Janet demanded.

'He can find his way back over this scrub — and he can take his chances if there are any more Mescalero around. He's a big boy; let him ride back to his ranch the way he came.'

Full of indignation, Janet bent close to Hertzog, who was glaring at Dane Lander.

'I'll see you again,' Janet whispered.

'You bet,' was the low reply. 'Your pa won't keep us apart. I'll find a way to git you out of that outlaw roost. It ain't right for you to live like that. You'd be better off living in Palermo with some friends.'

'I — I haven't many friends . . . '

'That I can understand. One girl among that pack o' no-goods,' he gritted. 'Your father has some crazy notions. Maybe it ain't much of my business — but what happened to your mother, Janet?'

She hesitated. Her father was watching them angrily. 'Dad never told me much — but — but my mother is dead — long before he came to the Yellow Hills. That's all I know.'

'Haven't you any pictures of her?'

'Nothing.' She moved restlessly, subdued by some inner thoughts. 'I only know that my mother was called Laura. Dad — he — he just doesn't talk about her to me.'

'It ain't natural,' Hertzog said. 'What sort of way is that to bring up a girl?'

'All right, you two!' Dane Lander, at the end of his patience, roared out the words. 'Let's move out, Janet!'

The riders set off again, and Hertzog angled into the afternoon sun, with many a backward glance until he was a speck on the horizon.

Tim Hara did his best to conceal his curiosity as they entered the Yellow Hills. First there was an obvious trail, with hoofmarks deep in the soft earth. This gave way to a defile that had a bed of clean hardrock and this, in turn, branched off into numerous clefts that were like passages. Tim wondered how they would gain access to the centre of the hills where the camp of the owlhoots was reputedly located. He was sure the trail would be well hidden, and maybe there was more than one way in. Another detail struck him which he'd known about: this hilly land could be defended by a handful of men. There were scores of natural lookout positions. Even now men might be watching. If it came to fighting, one concealed man could handle ten or even twenty attackers.

The horses picked their way down a defile so narrow that stirrups nearly touched the sides of the smooth yellow rock. The walls rose high and were topped by rounded cones. The pathway twisted and began to climb steeply, like a ramp, going diagonally up a cliff face.

Tim Hara guessed that their movement up this crevice could not be seen by anyone positioned on the approach trail. He was pretty sure now that this would be only one of a number of secret entrances to the fortress.

There were other surprises. The track led through a screen of shrubs and creepers into a cave. The roof had holes and clefts through which light came.

It seemed a long time to Tim Hara before the ride through the tunnel was over, then they entered a broad canyon dotted with cactus clumps. The party cantered along the sandy bottom for half a mile and then went through a rocky gorge of yellow rock which was the gateway to Lander's Kingdom.

Suddenly Tim Hara saw the camp. It lay in a natural bowl, the walls terraced like an ancient amphitheatre. He saw adobe buildings and horse corrals. An imposing house had been built into the natural rock. The frontage had many windows, curtained and painted white around the woodwork. There was a verandah, chairs, a bed of flowers.

The terraces were filled with cholla and mesquite scrub. Chaparral grew like clawing tentacles.

Tim dismounted near the main corral. He patted his horse and led it into the enclosure. There was feed and water. He wondered if he should unsaddle the animal.

He was utterly alone in this nest of

killers. If they suspected him, he was a goner. But his cover story might work for long enough. The gold should be convincing proof that he was on the run. And Luke Dugald would have put on a good show in Famoso. Soon the news of the posse hunt for him would get through to Lander's Kingdom.

He was busy with his horse when Dane Lander and two men approached. Their quick strides warned Tim. He swung around.

'You need to be taught a lesson, rannigan,' said the big man. 'I sentence you to forty-eight hours' detention for your insolence. At the end of that time you'll realize who's the master in this organisation. Take him away, men.'

4

Playing A Hunch

The cell was a rocky hole in a cliff face without a light or a window. There was no bed or comfort of any kind. A massive wooden door, built of planks from a discarded wagon, closed Tim in. He'd noticed on the way to the cell that there were similar doors in the cave-like passage.

The air was stale and warm, but, thankfully, it was cooler than outside. As the hours wore on, the warmth and lack of light made him drowsy. He figured the best way to beat forty-eight hours of this punishment was to sleep as much as possible.

He lay huddled in a corner and fell asleep. Hours later, he wakened, thirsty and with a hollow feeling in the pit of his stomach. His last meal had been breakfast early that morning, and he'd used up a lot of energy since.

He kicked at the door, shouting and demanding food and water. He stopped when his voice became a hoarse croak. He swallowed painfully and lay down again, then he brought out his pocket watch and carefully wound it, squinting in the dimness. The only light came from somewhere down the cave passage and trickled almost imperceptibly under the door and above it, where the joint allowed a few inches of space.

He didn't know how much time had passed. His watch said two o'clock. He thought it must be afternoon.

Escape was impossible. The door couldn't be forced open. Solid rock lay all around him. They had taken his guns and his Bowie knife. All his other gear was in his saddle-bags. And, of course, they had the gold. But that was the least of his worries. The gold had been deemed a necessary touch by General Charlton. As army men they were accustomed to obtaining men and materials — and the gold came under that category.

After more hours, Tim got up and began to walk around the cell, pacing like a trapped animal. He was now desperately in need of water. His tongue was swollen; his lips were thick. He needed food but he doubted if he could chew steak. He could do with some nourishing stew.

As he was walking slowly around the confined space, he heard small sounds outside the thick door. Then a peephole cover slid to one side. He realized there was a man outside — and a girl. Janet Lander.

Tim came to the door. 'Get me out of here,' he croaked.

'I can't,' she said. 'Dad won't agree. Oh, I tried. I know you helped John, and I — I'm sorry about some of the things I said about you.'

'They were true,' he said thickly. 'I'm a wanted man ... ' Even this girl mustn't suspect that he wasn't a no-good owlhoot.

'I know, but you did help John, and — well, I don't approve of this inhuman treatment.'

'Don't worry about me. I'll walk out of here, Miss Lander.' And then, for the benefit of the guard: 'I guess I made a big mistake comin' here with that gold. I should've made for the border . . . '

'I wish I could help you,' Janet said, 'but I can't. I can get into trouble with Dad just for being here — and this man, Midgeland, too. He's only doing it for me . . . '

Tim Hara sympathized with this girl and her troubled conscience. He'd been told about Lander's daughter, but only to the extent that she lived with her father in the outlaw fort. He hadn't been given any information about Janet as a person. That was the trouble with army reports; they were so damned impersonal. Janet Lander had problems and he could understand them. But he had no solution to offer. Besides, his job was to discover the secrets within Lander's Kingdom and to kill or capture Dane Lander.

The latter objective would have to be delayed to give him time to spy around this fortress. Of course, everything depended on his being accepted as a member of the outlaw gang.

' . . . wish I could do something for you,' Janet said.

He had to fight to get a smile on his puffed lips. 'It's all right.'

The peep-hole slid shut.

He had to wait it out, hold onto his strength. Forty-eight hours — it wasn't too much.

He wasn't surprised when he calculated that the forty-eight hours had ended and he still wasn't released.

Tim's watch told him he was well into the third day when the big cell door swung open and two men strode in. They were faceless rannigans to Tim Hara. He was dazed and weak and his mouth and throat were thick, harsh bits of flesh that rasped like sandpaper. He was led along the cave passage and into the morning sun. Tim screwed his eyes and stumbled along. There was no fight in him.

He was taken before Dane Lander in what reminded him of an army staff room. Lander sat like a general behind a big desk. The walls were hung with maps.

'Maybe you're in a better frame of mind now,' said the big man. He seemed cheerful, enjoying his authority. He was immaculate in a new plaid shirt and brown pants tucked into hand-made riding boots. The shirt stretched across his broad chest.

'I can barely stand up,' Tim muttered. 'You took my gold and stuck me in that damn cell. You figure that's the way to treat a feller who wants to work for you?'

Lander stuck out his chin. 'You committed the crime of insolence. But I'm a fair man. You've served your detention, and now we'll see what we can make of you.'

'You can start by bringing me some food and water. And I'd like my share of that gold,' Tim slurred out through his swollen lips.

'Still sassy!' Lander narrowed his eyes. 'Well, in a way I like that, Hara. A man without guts isn't of much use to me.' He laughed. 'I might need a good two-gun man pretty soon. I've got a little exploit planned that will require four top men.'

'Give me my gold and a bonus for this new job and I'm your man.' Speech was painful, but Tim figured he had to make an impression.

'You'll get your share of your gold,' Lander said. 'Now you can get some food and water. You have two hours and then you can start working for me by doing four hours of guard duty on Eagle's Roost.' Lander nodded to the two men. 'Take him to the bunkhouse.'

Minutes later, Tim drank cool water from a mug. Then a grinning negro came from the cookhouse with some food on a tin dish. It seemed to be mainly gravy, with rice, soft vegetables and tiny cubes of meat. Tim managed to get it down, then he looked into the black man's grinning face.

'Didn't think you could manage steak, buckeroo! Just ask Sam if you want some more of that!'

'I want more, Sam. Tastes real good . . . '

Later, he was shown a bunk. His saddle-bags were there, hanging from a nail. He looked through them and found his belongings intact. There wasn't much: moccasins, a spare bandanna, his fieldglasses, a purse with five dollars, two spare shirts and some socks and the picture of a girl (she was a saloon kid from San Antonio but that fact would matter to no one). He took out a long-handled razor, a piece of soap and his makings. Tim Hara liked to be clean-shaven. He rolled a cigarette and lit it, blowing smoke luxuriously. When the cigarette had burned away, he went to a corner of the bunkhouse and shaved. Suddenly he felt better. Now if he had his guns, he'd feel absolutely fine. Maybe he'd get them when he was 'trusted'.

An hour later he was shown his guard post, a craggy lookout high up in the wall around the natural basin. From there he had a perfect view of passes to the east of the hideout.

'Stick around here, *amigo*,' grinned the man who'd taken him up the almost perpendicular path. 'You'll be relieved in just four hours. But you won't see anybody — just a few buzzards flappin' around for a meal.'

Guard duty was another facet of Lander's discipline. Tim had no weapons. He sat out the time without seeing a thing. But he studied the lay of the land.

That night he slept on a bunkhouse bed. The ranny named Ralph tried in vain to rile him, then gave up and rolled into his blanket. An oldster with the long, mournful face and dark eyes of a half-breed Indian, tried to pump him and got the ready answers Tim felt he wanted to hear.

Darkness fell and there was silence

except for the sound of snoring. Twelve men shared the bunkhouse; there were probably another twelve in the second building. Warily watching, Tim Hara soon realised there was a roster of night guard duty for some. About midnight a man came in and another, reluctantly leaving his bunk, went into the cool night.

That was when Tim decided to start nosing around. He slipped out of the bunkhouse, moccasins on his feet, a dark shirt on his back.

He wasn't sure if he'd find anything of importance, but he had to start somewhere. His immediate task was to ascertain the rounds of the sentries, learn the position of dark shadows. The sliver of moon hung low and gave faint light. The air, after the heat of the day, was cool. He went along the side of the adobe bunkhouse, all senses alert. His stamina had returned.

Dane Lander's house lay silent. The way the place had been built into the rock face aroused his curiosity. Were there special reasons for making use of the rock face?

Silent as a stalking Indian, he slid around to the side of the house where the shadows were deep. This was, he reminded himself, just a preliminary scout around. Maybe he'd have to slink out for more than one night. Maybe he'd never discover a thing. Maybe he'd slip up and take a Colt slug in the head.

Already he strongly felt that anything of interest must lie in this house — unless there were caves elsewhere in Lander's Kingdom that he knew nothing about. The buildings seemed ordinary enough — the bunkhouses, the stores, a smoke-blackened black-smith's forge, a tack-room, a cookhouse. He had already spotted them. There wasn't any mystery about them. But the house . . .

He reached a door on the side. The round knob didn't turn.

He searched around, found a thin length of chaparral twig and returned to the door. A man in the frontier lived largely on hunches. Sometimes they landed him in trouble. Maybe this would, but he had to follow it up.

He used the twig as a lever in the hole in the door. After a few attempts he felt a catch lift. Slowly, he pressed on the door. It swung in an inch without a squeak.

The door gave way to a dark passage. He splayed a hand over the nearest wall. Rock. It was cool. The passage was as dark as a mine. He was somewhere near the back of Lander's house, at a point where the building faced into the natural rock. What he wanted was access to the man's papers — any documents or books he kept.

A look along this passage would do for a start. Soon he saw a touch of light at the far end of this rock-faced passage. He sidled along, thinking he must be deep into the rock by now. It seemed the house led into a system of caves. He was sure of this idea when the passage came to a junction. Two shafts went off in a 'Y' and another went back, at an angle to the one he'd used. He guessed that it would lead into the centre of the house. A lantern was burning in a chiselled-out alcove. He could smell the oil. Why light the place?

There could be only one answer. The passages were used.

He debated whether to push on or beat a retreat. He felt at a loss without his guns. He hesitated, something he seldom did. He always considered action — even careless impulse — better than nail-chewing. A man could always fight back if things went wrong. So he chose the passage on his right and the hell with it.

He went about five yards past the central, lantern-lit junction — and then froze as he heard footsteps. One pair of boots rasped on rock. Somewhere a man was trudging along.

The sound had travelled a good distance, he realized a few moments later; then, after a minute or so he saw a bobbing light. The walker was far down the passage.

Tim Hara saw the only depression in the rockface of the passage wall that could hide him, but it wouldn't afford any concealment at all when the man came abreast of him.

He held his breath and waited. Another few seconds and the yellow glow from the lantern would light up his hiding place.

He had to act.

Before the man could properly see him, he went surging out in a swift leap that brought him against the man. The lantern fell and rolled but didn't go out. The man gasped and tried to snarl a challenge. Tim Hara hit him before the man could get a good look at him; he didn't want someone who could identify him later.

The man took the blow between the eyes and fell with a dull thud to the passage floor. Tim stared down at a horse-like face. Another drifter from God knew where, he thought. A damned nuisance!

Then Tim Hara saw the tray that had

fallen with the lantern. He picked it up and looked curiously at it. Tiny drops of food still clung to it. Part of the tray was still warm.

He had to get rid of this man. If he left him, he'd come around and raise a rumpus. Tim picked up the lantern and tucked the tray under his arm. With his right hand he grasped the unconscious man by the shirt and began to haul him along the passage like a sack of spuds.

The man had been feeding someone or maybe he'd been having a snack somewhere. But why eat in these tunnels? It was a bit odd.

The passage turned and he saw another lantern burning in a wall niche. There was something else; a metal grille was fixed across the tunnel. He examined the iron bars, noting they were firmly cemented into holes in the rockface. There was a small door which was held closed by a large padlock.

He found a large metal key in the man's trousers pocket. He took it and turned the padlock. He left the lock hanging in position, but open, after he'd gone through the grille. He dragged the limp body along and still carried the lantern and tray.

The tunnel became high-domed, taking on the natural contours of a cave. He climbed a craggy series of ledges with the idea of getting rid of the tray in some cranny. Then he discovered the hole.

Even with the aid of the lantern he couldn't see to the bottom of this round, shaft-like pit. He dropped a stone into it. Seconds passed before it hit bottom.

He returned to the man. He was coming around. He was going to be a nuisance all right. If Tim left him here he'd be at Dane Lander's side as quickly as he could walk there. That might mean grief, although he was sure the fellow could not identify him.

The grim way out of the situation was now obvious with the discovery of the hole.

He dragged the body up the high,

uneven wall until he reached the pit again. Savage lines of distaste were etched into Tim Hara's face as he rolled the body into the shaft. A long pause, then came the final thud . . .

'Heaven help me,' he muttered. 'But it was you or me, friend.'

He reached the tunnel again and went on quickly. Moments later he came to a big wooden door which barred the way. The door was near a dark tunnel which, he figured, went on into the cliff. Looking down the tunnel, he saw that it was utterly black. The door, on the other hand, showed signs of use. The hinges were greased and the post on the left showed scratches.

Curious, he tried the key he'd taken from the man. It didn't fit the padlock. Swearing, he realized the man probably had another key on him somewhere. Tim moved his lantern close to the half-inch of space around the door edge and tried to peer through. For a few moments he squinted uncertainly into some sort of lighted room beyond but wasn't able to define anything.

All at once, in the cold silence of the cave, he heard a low moaning and then a monotonous chanting of some gibberish. There was a pause, then an unexpected peal of laughter. It was a woman's laughter — maniacal laughter!

5

Rustler's Trail

In the bunkhouse Tim Hara lay thinking . . .

He'd been unable to pick the lock on the big wooden door. Without a key, he'd need a crowbar or a charge of explosives to open the door.

He'd heard the chilling laughter and didn't doubt it came from a woman. Who was she? And why did Lander keep her locked away? He had his suspicions, but only a face-to-face encounter with the woman behind that solid door would solve the mystery. Maybe there would be another chance, another day. But the problems he faced were tremendous. However, this was no time for worrying. Tim Hara closed his eyes and fell asleep.

The next morning he met Dirk

Schulman. The large, solidly built man marched into the bunkhouse as the men were preparing for the day. Some were washing and dressing and others were eating at tables where Sam, the negro, placed breakfast.

Dirk Schulman's bald, round head was the colour of old leather. His small eyes were fringed above with tufty red brows. His mouth was a wide slit. He wore a flapping deerskin vest. He'd taken it from a man he'd killed a long way back. His pride was a walrus moustache of the same fiery red as his eyebrows.

He came to Tim. 'The name's Dirk Schulman. I'm the boss's tophand. Next to Lander what I says goes — git it?'

Tim Hara smiled. 'Sure.'

'Lander says you're for guard duty again — down in the foothills. You'll pair with Sid Minton — that's the runt over there.' Schulman indicated a small man in a washed-out shirt and black pants sizes too big for him.

'When do I git some real riding?' Tim drawled. 'I mean doin' a job on a bank or a stage.'

'I think Lander has something arranged,' Schulman said. 'Don't prod, mister. I hear you just done some time in the hoosegow.'

'I've been in worse.'

Schulman poked a big finger against Tim's chest. 'I wasn't here yesterday, so I ain't seen much of you, *amigo*. You ain't in the clear as yet, but you might be after you do what Lander has cooked up for you . . . '

'What about my guns? You expect me to work without guns?'

'You can pick up a rifle for the guard duty.'

A bit later, he was taking a look at his corralled horse when he heard some men talking.

'Seems that bum who works in the house vamoosed last night,' said one.

'You mean he ran off?'

'He ain't anywheres around. The boss is kinda het up this morning. I heard him stampin' about, tellin' that Chink cook he wasn't fit to live!'

'Aw, that bum musta lifted some booze and took off. He'll be back — unless he got himself a horse.'

'We're checking that right now.'

Tim turned and walked away. Minutes later he and the runty man went through the cave and out to lookout positions that gave them a clear view of the desert for miles around. Perched up in the rocks, they could see clear along the trail to Famoso and Palermo. At each position a large, round brass disc hung from a string on scrub. Tim examined his disc and noted the bullet scars. Sid Minton called out:

'That's the alarm. Two shots into the brass and it echoes through the hills. Last time it was a posse. But they don't ride this way any more. We killed three in the posse and winged a few more.'

'What about one rider? Like that one.' Tim pointed to the tiny speck of black that barely showed on the heat-hazed horizon.

Sid shaded his eyes and tried in vain to spot something. 'You ain't foolin'? I can't see anythin'.'

'Then just sit down on that bony backside and wait,' said Tim calmly. 'There's a man in black, riding slowly this way.' He stared and added thoughtfully. 'Seems like he knows his direction. Lander expecting any visitors?'

'How in hell should I know? I'm just another gunhand. You think the boss tells me anything except mount up and go git down there shootin'?'

'Ain't no way to treat a man,' Tim said. 'Tell me — does Dane Lander ever have any women come to the fort?'

'Nope. Ain't no women allowed — except that daughter of his, of course. A man wants a woman, he's got to get permission to ride to town.'

'That's a bit tough on a man,' Tim said.

'I tell you, Lander don't like skirts. I seen the way he treats 'em and I could tell you plenty.'

'Well, Sid, you go right ahead. I'm mighty curious.'

'I ain't talkin' no more. I don't trust you. Come to that, I don't trust anybody on this damn place. They're always tryin' to put one over on me . . . '

Tim Hara looked towards the horizon again. 'That rider is kind of small — like you, Sid, and dressed in black. Now who would fit that description?'

The little man spent a long time watching the approaching horseman before he gave his opinion. 'Aw, that's that snaky gink from Famoso. I seen him ride in here. Lawyer Baily, that's him.'

'I don't know him.' Tim was thoughtful. Anyone who came from Famoso since Dugald's ride into the ramshackle town could be significant.

'He's a snake but the boss-man likes to hear him talk. I guess he peddles a few secrets. He don't pack a gun — unless he has a derringer.'

'I take it we don't sound any alarm?'

'Hell, no. He'll find his way in.'

Tim Hara had to be content with a waiting game. Soon the small man in black rode sedately through the gully and vanished.

Some time later the white-haired little man with the serene smile was comfortably seated in Dane Lander's house, a glass of whisky in his hand. Lander watched him from another chair.

'I've got news for you about the big herd down at Palermo,' Baily said. 'They're getting ready for a drive to Sansemo. You asked me about that herd the last time I was here.'

'Yep. There are cattle buyers a bit nearer than the railroad at Sansemo.'

'You mean the miners at Pecos River?'

'I do, Mr. Baily. They need meat.'

The small man chuckled. 'They're not supposed to be mining near the river, are they, Mr. Lander? That is Indian Territory and they have no right to be there.'

'That's a damn fool law!'

'I agree.' Baily smiled. 'Yes, they need meat and will pay handsomely for it.' Lawyer Baily leaned over the table and helped himself to a cigar. He enjoyed these little tête-à-têtes with Lander; it made him feel important.

'First I have to get the beef,' Lander said.

'You'd be wise to act within twenty-four hours,' said the little man. 'The cattle are herded in a valley just outside Palermo. What with the big fiesta planned for the next two days, there won't be many men watching the herd. You could take part of it without any trouble at all.'

'And then all we'd have to do is drive the beef up to Halligan's ranch just outside Palermo,' Lander said. 'He has two box canyons on his land where the beef could be hidden.'

Baily nodded. 'The cattle could reach Halligan's place before any posse could catch up with it. He has plenty of beef which could be used to foul up the trail.

A greedy man, Halligan.'

'But useful — at the moment.' Dane Lander blew out cigar smoke reflectively. 'Yes, it could work. Five hundred head discreetly trail-driven a week or so later to the miners on the Indian Territory would pay off nicely. At least it would keep my men busy and pay them some dinero.'

'Well, no one else will sell the miners meat in the quantity they need.' Lawyer Baily sipped at his drink and stretched. He looked like a benign little preacher in his black frock-coat. 'Hungry men — miners.' He leaned forward and took a sheet of paper from his pocket. 'Sheriff Luke Dugald chased a man into Famoso recently — a wanted man. Seems he stole some gold, but he didn't come into Famoso. Here's a wanted poster of this man. He might still be hiding out in the badlands with his gold — and you might come across him.'

Dane Lander examined the picture and the description of Tim Hara with some interest. He gave a laugh of satisfaction.

'The man is right here, enjoying the security of my fort. As for his gold, it's in safe custody.' He tapped the bill. 'I'll keep this. Thanks. Seems this *hombre* is just the kind of man I need. I've been watching him, naturally — and I had to punish him — but for some reason I like the hardcase. Strange, isn't it, how seldom you meet a man you feel you could be friendly with?'

'It is,' said Lawyer Baily smoothly. He had long since lost interest in anything but a quick financial return. 'So you'll go for the cattle? And I can expect a little commission?'

'Sure. Now I'll leave you to enjoy a meal. Hoo Chung will look after you.'

Dane Lander had some plans to make. He went to see Dirk Schulman.

'Get ready to ride a few hours before sundown tonight, Schulman. We're heading for a little rustling in a valley near Palermo. Tell Ralph to get fixed up with ropes — he's a handy galoot with cows, I'm told. You'll want bedrolls and water. I'm going with you and I'll try out that new man, Tim Hara. Give him his guns and get him briefed. We'll need a few more men — I'll leave that to you.' Dane Lander looked out the window. 'I'll tell you more later about this beef we're after.'

When Dirk Schulman had gone, Lander went to the rear of his rambling house. He walked down a passage, opened a door and stared thoughtfully along a tunnel of natural rock. Why did he feel compelled to make this visit every day? There were swift, violent ways of dealing with most troubles, but this was something that had tortured him for a long time.

Was there any way of ridding himself of this burden? Would he ever experience a day when he didn't think about it? He had killed and plundered without compunction, but this — this scar on his mind — what could he do about it?

He walked slowly down the tunnel, opened the iron grille and went on, a big man, his shoulders hunched just a little.

He heard the wild laughter long before he reached the big wooden door and the lantern that burned continually. He tried to shut out the sound from his ears. Damn it! Why didn't he end it?

Dane Lander opened the heavy door and swung it back on its greased hinges. It struck him briefly that he'd have to get another keeper; the other idle swine had apparently taken off.

Then a wild female cry greeted him and he shouted desperately, 'Quiet! Quiet, you — you damned torment!'

* * *

Tim Hara finished his spell of guard duty and returned to the bunkhouse. He saw men leisurely attending to various chores. Then, after a rough but stomach-filling meal, he was confronted by Dirk Schulman.

'Feller, you can get your guns.'

'That's mighty good of you.' Tim

scrutinized the round face and the beady eyes. 'Did Lander say anything about that blasted gold of mine?'

'He's got ridin' work for you. Tonight — just afore sundown. Pin your ears back, hombre . . . '

They rode out that night, going in single file through the gullies that led to the fort — six men: Lander, Schulman, Ralph, Tim and two hard-looking saddlebums whose names Tim didn't know or care to know. The sun would set in two hours and then darkness would fall swiftly, as it did in this land. They would ride the best part of the way to Palermo and then camp somewhere off the trail and get some rest. Then they would hit the grazing herd early in the morning. The plan had been outlined to Tim Hara by Dirk Schuman. He had to go along and play the role of a rustler to the hilt. Life sure got mixed up at times, he thought. He'd renounced lawlessness and as a result of the bargain he'd made with Captain Morgan and the federal town marshal from Sansemo, he was now part of an outlaw band. And he'd killed.

Dane Lander was silent and looked oddly thoughtful until they made camp some ten miles out of Palermo. Then, as Tim Hara smoked a last cigarette, Lander walked to him and brought out his own smokes, a machine-made product that was rare on the frontier.

'You don't really gab much,' Lander said, watching Tim's face.

'At times I do.'

'But you don't really say much.'

'Now what the heck is that supposed to mean?'

Lander smiled. 'I know you gunhands have plenty to hide, but I've known some who boast. Takes all kinds, I reckon. Did you say you were known down San Antonio way?'

'Sure. I like San Antonio.'

'Killed a man down there, didn't you?'

'How do you know that?'

'Well, I've got ways of discovering facts about men. You're wanted in West Texas.'

'Sure. That's why your camp suits me.'

Lander abruptly changed the topic. 'Ever get married? Has there ever been a woman?'

Tim Hara blew smoke and lowered his gaze. 'There have been women — I got a picture of one right now.' He felt in his shirt pocket where he had placed the picture of the saloon girl after taking it from his saddle-bag.

Lander glanced at it, drawing on his cigarette, the red glow illuminating the grainy photograph. 'She's good-looking.'

'Do you allow women in the fort?' Tim asked.

'No!' The answer came sharply. 'No women!'

'Hard on some galoots who fancy a look-see at petticoats.'

'It's a rule.'

'Hard on yourself, too,' suggested Tim, his narrowed eyes taking in Lander's reactions.

'I can do without them.' There was

bitterness in Lander's voice.

'But you allow Janet to live in the hills.'

Lander moved restlessly. He had initiated the conversation on a friendly level but it wasn't going his way. He'd hoped to talk to Tim Hara about general topics, seeking some intelligent conversation about the state of the country, the tremendous drive by the railroads, the cattle barons in the new territories and the role of the U.S. Army. But somehow the talk had veered around to women — of all subjects!

'She hasn't been in Yellow Hills more than three years. Before that she lived in Abilene.'

'She likes living in the fort with nothin' around but men and horses?'

'It was her wish. But I have a feeling she'll have to return to Abilene.'

'To her mother?'

'Her mother is dead.'

'Well, that figures. I mean she wouldn't like her girl living in an outlaw roost. That's the way of women.'

Dane Lander drew himself up and stamped on the butt of his cigarette. 'I'd hoped to have some sort of conversation with you, Hara, but you seem bent on asking fool questions. Goodnight!'

Tim grinned as the big man walked back to his bedroll. A bit later he had made himself comfortable, with saddle-bags and guns within reach. The pale moon cast its weak light over the camp and the tethered horses. Tim knew that Ralph was watching him. He'd seen him talking to Lander and evidently he didn't like it.

'Hope you can trail-herd steers, partner,' he sneered. 'It's hard work — somethin' the usual two-gun man kinda hides from!'

'Don't rile me,' Tim said. 'If we hit trouble you might be glad I pack two hoglegs.'

Tim rolled onto his side and went to sleep. For a long time, Ralph's eyes drilled into his back . . . eyes that glowed with hate.

6

The Thunderbolt

The six men awakened early and made a quick breakfast of beans and bacon over trail fires. They burned old sticks and mesquite roots, and the smoke hung in the lifeless air. It was going to be another warm day, humid, tinder-dry, with the cholla cactus and the Joshua trees digging their roots another fraction of an inch deeper in search of moisture. They ate, the rannigans telling rough jokes, mainly about women they'd known.

Tim Hara watched Ralph at intervals. He sensed the man's animosity just as surely as he knew the menace of a pointed sixgun. So Ralph hated him. Well, it was too bad.

Lander was the first to be ready. His big black was frisky the moment he felt the weight of the saddle.

They rode for the valley outside Palermo as the sun rose over the hills.

It was a characteristic of West Texas that the nature of the land changed every few miles, and they could see this as they rode. Suddenly there was gramma grass and tufts of wild green bunch grass. The chaparral clumps were more infrequent. They came close to the first of the big spreads near Palermo and avoided detection; it was early even for hard-working punchers to be around.

They saw a small herd of cattle under the first clump of cottonwoods they encountered. One group of cattle stood in a dried-up creek; another bunch nosed for browned grass under some mesquite. However, what they wanted was the big herd, secure in a valley and waiting for the big push to Sansemo and the railroad.

They reached the ridge overlooking the long, slow slope that led to the peaceful herd. The cattle stretched for a mile down the sheltered valley, searching for anything edible. There wouldn't be much grass left after two days. Dane Lander got the men together and punched his words home: 'We hit them now! I can't see a puncher anywhere! If you meet some hell-fired guy, gun him down! The others will run. That suits us. While they're away looking around for help we can get going to Halligan's place. If we drive the cattle hard we can make it, hide the stock and then ride off. Everybody got it?'

They nodded and grunted.

'Remember, I want the stock moving fast.'

'I can push cows like all hell,' Ralph said. He gave Tim a sneering glance. 'Ain't so sure about some others, though.'

'All right, Mr Lander, we've got it,' said Dirk Schulman. 'These jiggers will work under me. You don't have to drive steers.'

'I'm riding with you all the same.'

They went loping into the valley,

quietly, efficiently, ropes lashing the hides of the nearest cattle. They got them moving in bunches, prodding them into speed. There was inevitably some noise as the cattle started bellowing and hoofs drummed at the earth.

A ranchhand appeared on a horse, riding out of a rocky nook where he'd been dozing in the saddle. 'Hey, what the hell! What's this?'

He rode uncertainly towards the dirty-faced, unshaven Ralph. Ralph turned his horse and drew his sixgun.

For a few moments Ralph stared at the oncoming man. The puncher was still bemused with sleep. Then, when he saw the gun, awareness hit him. With a cry of fear he turned his animal and rammed his spurs to it.

But Ralph's gun spoke once and the puncher slowly toppled from his saddle, agony contorting his face. One boot remained in a stirrup and he was dragged along by his frightened horse until he hit a rock and his foot came free.

Tim Hara had watched the back-shooting incident with compressed lips. He'd remember that the hellion wasn't too particular about the West's unwritten code that gave a man the chance to draw — face to face.

The shot and the bawling of the cattle had been noticed farther down the valley and two riders came at the gallop to investigate. When they saw the strangers working on the herd, they drew their guns; then, as they neared handgun range, they threw accurate lead. But it wasn't good enough. Lander's gunnies, riding fast at the punchers, used their guns with terrible effect. The two cowhands fell from their mounts and lay still. Their horses wheeled away in fright.

Tim Hara had one gun clear of leather. His roan was close to a bunch of running steers, head turned. There was nothing he could do. He turned the prancing roan and lashed out with a rope at some cattle that showed sign of veering away. When he looked around again Ralph was close to him.

'You use that hogleg?'

'Wasn't any need. You seemed to be doin' all the gun-toting.'

'That was the order.'

'All right, partner, so that was the order. You did fine. What the hell are you crowdin' me for?'

It was just another little incident showing Ralph's animosity towards him. The man was signalling his future intentions; a fool thing, Tim thought.

The shooting had the effect of deterring a few *vaqueros* down the valley. They sat their horses at a distance, then rode off. Obviously they realised what was going on and didn't like the odds.

Dane Lander and his outfit got the cattle moving fast out of the valley and then on a trail that would take them to the broken country where Halligan's ranch lay.

They shouted and yipped at the scared cattle, thrashing any rump within reach and continually urging them on. After an hour or more of sweating, cursing and hard riding, they came within sight of the Halligan ranch.

Two riders came out to meet them — a Mexican in a steeple-shaped hat and a fat man with a frowsy moustache. After some shouts between the two men and Dirk Schulman, the herd was sent towards the range of low, broken hills that surrounded Halligan's ranch. The cattle were pushed unmercifully, almost at stampede haste. The drumming hoofs took the beasts through a twisting defile and into a box canyon mouth and the sandy bed was swept with scrub branches. Halligan would run some of his own cattle near the broken hills as camouflage. The stolen cattle would remain in the hidden canyon until it was time to move them again.

Dane Lander, watching the horizon for signs of pursuit, rode to Halligan, a dark-haired, dark-eyed man of obvious Celtic origin. They exchanged comments and then, their work completed, the outlaws turned their hardworked horses for the arid lands. It seemed that Dane Lander had pulled off a neat little bit of business that would bring in some useful profit for himself and his followers. The five hundred head was a bread-and-butter deal obtained at no loss and little more than twenty-four hours of hard riding.

Tim Hara stared into the sky and noted the stillness, the lack of air movement. The sun was rising still, like a brassy orb, and the whole land seemed like an oven. The horses plodded steadily, their riders slumped, glad that the exertion was over.

Hours later they were deep into the badlands. Suddenly the sky changed colour. Clouds gathered quickly, moving in on currents of air that gained speed as hot air was sucked upwards. The obscured sun glared eerily through the thickening cloud. The silent air hung hot and ominous over the slow-moving horses.

'Looks like a thunderstorm brewing,'

said Tim Hara to Dane Lander.

As the tall outlaw chief nodded, Ralph said sneeringly, 'It's devil's brew! I seen it afore. Rain and thunder! I seen a man killed by lightnin' once. I figger it's the devil a-pickin' his own . . . '

'It's electricity in the air,' said Tim calmly. 'The devil exists only in men . . . '

Ralph contorted his face. 'Yeah — you know it all, huh? I tell you I seen the devil pick out a jasper and burn him into a cinder. That's the way I see it — not this — this — what do you call it?'

'Electricity.'

'Ain't no such thing, mister! It's devil's work. I reckon some feller is gonna die.'

'You talk like a fool!' Dane Lander rapped out. 'Hara is right. Electricity is everywhere, in the rocks and in the sky, and one day man will use it to power his machines. I've read a lot about the subject in some Boston journals. Our use of this remarkable power, such as in the telegraph, is only in its infancy.'

Tim Hara shot the man a glance. Here again was a glimpse of the intelligence of this renegade. Strange that he'd decided to live outside the law.

Ralph scowled and sent another glance at the varicoloured sky. Reds and blacks swirled threateningly. The man rubbed a dirty bandanna over his face and muttered, 'Devil's brew, I say! Ain't nothin' else! Maybe it'll strike soon!'

The riders and horses were uneasy. All at once the still desert air was broken by a vivid flash of lightning and a sharp crack of thunder. In the next moment huge drops of rain pelted down. Controlling their snorting mounts, the men looked up at the sky.

'Rain I can take,' grunted Dirk Schulman. 'But that damn lightning scares me.'

'The devil's reachin' out!' Ralph bawled. 'I reckon he's fixin' to teach some jigger a lesson!'

'Could be you, mister,' said one rider.

Ralph gave him a nasty glance. 'I

figure it's the stranger. Yeah, the devil takes his own!'

'You certainly have an ignorant mouth,' Tim said.

The black sky swirled and eddied into a patch of crimson cloud and then the electrical storm discharged its power again. Lightning flashed its sharp blue light and thunder broke a second later. Rain fell with increasing intensity, streaking down the flanks of the horses and wetting the hats of the riders. Tim Hara turned up his face and felt the welcome wetness on his cheeks. The air was noticeably cooler. This freak storm would pass quickly, moving away on currents of air high in the sky. He'd experienced these storms before.

Tim turned his head after his remark about Ralph's ignorance. So Ralph's approach on a jigging horse and his clawing arms were unexpected. The first Tim Hara knew about it was when arms gripped around his chest and neck and tried to drag him from the saddle.

The move succeeded. Both men fell

to the ground, Tim's back ramming the earth. Ralph's grip held tight. In seconds, Tim was choking for breath. He instinctively grabbed the man's wrists but couldn't loosen the killing, vice-like grip.

Tim had to act fast while there was breath still in his body. He changed tactics and rammed his two fists into Ralph's middle.

The blow made Ralph buckle and his strangling hands loosened involuntarily. The few seconds of relief were valuable. Fast as a striking mountain cat, Tim Hara thrust at his opponent's wrists, while Ralph was still sick from the first blow. Tim prised the hands away and then he rolled, taking Ralph with him. For some seconds the two men scrambled in the dust while raindrops fell like great globules around them. Lander and the others stared with mixed expressions. Schulman grinned and another hardcase watched curiously. The heavens at that moment seemed to open up as more thunder and lightning tore through the swirling clouds, and the rain came down in a deluge.

Tim jerked to his feet and as Ralph straightened up he swung a right hand at him. Ralph, on the move, rode out the blow. Tim moved in with another hefty punch, a right swing that Ralph evaded just before he kicked out with both feet, his boots connecting with Tim's legs. Tim grimaced in agony, then his swinging fists landed on the other man's face but they lacked steam. Tim staggered, almost lame with the pain in his shins. But he came back angrily, hopping on one foot, his fists ramming at Ralph's lean face. The punches hit the target solidly and Ralph staggered back, his eyes glazing before he hit the dirt.

Tim rubbed his knuckles as he stared down at the prone man, then he moved stiffly for his horse. As he straddled leather, Ralph stirred. He rolled on the wet earth and sat up, his soiled range clothes collecting a layer of mud. He stared up at Tim Hara, all the hate in him showing in his twisted face. Then Dane Lander shouted impatiently:

'Cut out this damned wrangling! We've got a long way to go. This storm is lucky for us — it'll obliterate our tracks — but we're wasting time. I'll jail the next man who throws a punch!'

The threat was wasted on Ralph. He swore lustily and drew his gun.

Tim had turned his horse and didn't see the play. But a man shouted, 'Look out!'

Tim whipped around in the saddle, his hand clawing for his gunbutt.

Then there was a terrible noise, as if the heavens were falling apart. Blue light streaked down to the big sixgun in Ralph's hand. For a few awful seconds there was an unearthly howl of agony from Ralph's twisted mouth and his whole body contorted. There was the smell of burning flesh as the lightning played eerily around the gun for a moment.

Ralph's body fell lifelessly. His face was black and charred, his hair burned. Skin peeled back from his wrists and the gun was stuck fast to bone and grilled flesh.

'Hell and damnation — it got him!' Dirk Schulman, awe in his voice, backed his horse away.

'Him — and he figured the devil was after some other waddy!' cried another outlaw.

A fresh curtain of rain spat at the greedy earth and soaked the riders. Dane Lander was the first to recover from the fear that had claimed all.

'Let's get going! He was just unlucky, that's all.'

'Maybe he was right,' growled Dirk Schulman. 'Maybe the devil did take his own.'

'Cut out that stupid talk, Schulman. You know better than that! The lightning struck his gun, that's all. It's a thousand to one chance but it can happen.'

'I heard about it happening to a

galoot standing under some scrub trees,' said an outlaw. 'Yep — down in Arizona.'

'Move!' snapped Dane Lander and he pointed a gloved hand. It was an order and the four men obeyed it.

Tim Hara hunched in his saddle as his roan moved ahead. The sky was full of strange lights, making the horizon a vague smudge that seemed to change appearance every few minutes. The rain hissed at them. They passed a number of tall Joshua trees and then a rocky ridge. For some time even Lander was unsure of his bearings, then the light slowly returned to normal. The sun broke through the cloud and air currents dispersed the other clouds quickly. In minutes the storm clouds disappeared and the hot sun burned down as before. Only the clinging shirts on the backs of the men testified to the cloudburst.

'That Ralph sure got it good,' said Dirk Schulman, working his horse close to Tim's roan. 'Now why'n hell was he so on the prod with you, *amigo*?'

'We just didn't like each other.'

'Yeah? Anything else?'

Tim grinned back. 'You know how it is. A rannigan just takes a dislike to another feller. Now you and me, *compadre*, I guess we'll get along fine.'

'Yeah . . . maybe we will.' Dirk Schulman's beady eyes were reflective. He stroked his wet moustache, then he said in a voice so low that Tim guessed he didn't want Lander to overhear: 'You still annoyed about that gold?'

'Sure. It's rightly mine . . . '

The other nodded. 'Yep . . . sure seems to me you're takin' it mighty calm. How much d'you figure them bags are worth?'

'I never got around to valuing it.'

'Well, I heard some talk and I reckon that gold must be worth over two thousand dollars.'

'Could be so.'

'That's a neat bit of *dinero*. A man could live high on that for some time. You must be real sore about losin' it.'

'I get half,' said Tim quickly.

'Yeah?' Dirk Schulman spoke even lower. 'You mightn't get even that.'

'You figure he'd cheat me?'

The piggy eyes fastened on Tim Hara. 'What do you think?'

'I think I'll take my chances with Dane Lander,' said Tim Hara coolly.

Staring at the steam rising from the ground ahead, he wondered where this conversation was leading. Was Dirk Schulman trying to tell him something? Was the man trying to suggest some plan to retrieve the gold? Or was it all a trick to sound him out? Maybe Lander had put him up to it.

7

Confused By A Girl

After the evening meal in the bunk-house, Tim Hara sauntered around the basin which was the heart of Lander's Kingdom and smoked a rolled cigarette. He stopped to look at some half-wild mustangs in a corral, and was appraising a wiry animal when he saw the girl approach him.

He turned, took off his hat and smiled. 'Howdy, Miss Janet.'

She looked at Tim's tanned, clean-shaven face, then at the fresh clothes he'd donned right after arriving back at the hideout. His boots had been greased and polished, but he still had his stained stetson. Wonder about this drifter entered her mind. He hadn't been content to lounge around the bunkhouse with trail-dirt still on him.

Most of the men here accepted dust and sweat like it was a second skin. To them, soap and water were for use only on special occasions. She looked into Tim's eyes again.

'Aren't you tired after all that riding?'

'Maybe; a bit anyhow.' He grinned. 'You know, your father thinks of everything — he's even got a store. That's where I bought these new clothes. Seems I've got some credit.'

'The gold,' she said distantly. 'The gold you stole . . . '

'Could be that.' He decided to challenge her. 'You accept the food and shelter here — how do you justify that?'

'I don't.' Her blue eyes returned his gaze steadily.

A very desirable girl, he thought, even in blue jeans and a man's shirt. He was acutely aware of her womanly figure and he wondered how the outlaws kept their hands off her. Fear of Lander was probably the main reason.

Janet sighed. 'I wish I could leave this place with Dad. I've often tried to persuade him to disband this bunch and ride over the border — or any place where we could make a new life.'

'He enjoys his power,' said Tim Hara. 'You should sure know that by now.'

Her eyes faltered under his stare. 'Yes . . . but I — well, I just keep on hoping.'

'He'll die with a slug in him,' Tim said harshly. 'You should know that, too.'

'Are you going out of your way to be horrible?'

'I'm downright mean!' He grinned. When Tim Hara showed amusement, his dark eyes lost their wariness. Then his face sobered. 'I think you ought to get out of here. How about that aunt of yours in Abilene?'

'I still hope I might persuade Dad to go . . .'

'He'll die! Your pa will die at the end of a gun!' Tim checked his anger and added in a gentler tone: 'It could happen any time.'

'You seem to enjoy emphasising that point!' She turned, angry again. 'Why are you so concerned? You'd just find a new boss if my father died.'

'Maybe.' He was cautious again. 'It's just that you're young and — well, mighty pretty . . . '

Suddenly there was a strange expression in her eyes. She flicked a taunting glance over him, then curved her lips to reveal small white teeth. 'I'm pretty, am I? I thought you'd missed that.'

Tim was wise in the ways of the trail and the moods of a horse, but he had much to learn about women. Janet Lander came closer and the scent of her perfume filled his head. The evening breeze lifted her blonde hair and gently waved it over his lean cheek. His mind swirled with a sudden confusion that not even the perils of the trail could create. For a moment he stood there, feeling stupid and uncertain. She smiled like a child, her tanned skin flawless, her lips so near, so inviting . . .

'I am pretty, aren't I?'

It was a challenge and he knew it. 'You are — darned pretty,' he admitted.

Then, as if it were the most natural thing in the world, he held her shoulders lightly and kissed her on the mouth.

He thought she kissed him back, that her full mouth moved under his lips, but he couldn't be sure. The kiss lasted only a few moments and then he drew back, releasing her.

'I am young and pretty,' she said tauntingly, 'and you, Tim Hara, are a strange man. Thank you for the kiss, sir. At least now I know you're a friend and not an enemy.'

He watched her walk away, back to the big house fitted snugly into the strange caves of the cliff face. A house of mystery. It was time for another probe into the house that was Lander's personal residence. Maybe he could do it tonight. He hadn't all the time in the world. He was among the outlaws on false pretences and his role as a gun for hire could fall apart at any moment.

He walked slowly, with no real direction, deep in thought. The feel of her soft lips against his still lingered in his mind. She had been playing with him, he thought. He was so much older. And then there was John Hertzog.

Tim Hara was unaware that a man had seen the fleeting kiss. Dirk Schulman moved away from the tack-room window, a thoughtful hunch to his wide shoulders. His round face was inscrutable, but his eyes glinted. He could speak to Lander — but that wasn't so smart. Sure, he could have that clever two-gun guy thrown back into the hoosegow. But maybe it would pay to watch him for a bit longer. Pay in more ways than one . . .

Meals were something that Sam slung in the bunkhouse, but if a man wanted more food he could cook it himself. Tim Hara, feeling peckish, went into the cookhouse.

'Mind if I rustle up some chow?' he asked Sam.

'You can help yourself.' Sam indicated a side of bacon and a huge frying pan and resumed his indolent scrubbing of the preparation bench. 'Ain't no limit on grub in this outfit!'

'That's real good,' Tim drawled. 'You been with the boss long?'

'Me, suh?' Sam shook his head vaguely. 'Me — I ain't been out this place since ah came. Ah just keeps on dishin' up this grub and ah leaves the ridin' and shootin' to them other cusses.'

'Do you cook for Mr. Lander?'

'Sure do. But not all the time, no, suh. He got that Chinaman to serve up fancy stuff.'

'Yeah, feller name of Hoo Chung,' Tim muttered. 'So you just cook for the bunkhouse mainly?'

'Ah do prime steak for Mr Lander sometimes,' said Sam.

'But the Chink cooks mainly for the house?'

'Sure, but — '

'Mr Lander ain't got a wife. Just that daughter of his in that big house. Now why do they need a Chink cook just for

107

two people, Sam?'

'I dunno! Maybe they just like fancy food?'

'Could be.' Tim grinned. 'Have you ever spoken much to the Chink?'

'Nope. He just sticks around that house, man — like ah stick around this place. Mr Lander don't like us snoopin' around, man — don't you know that?'

Tim Hara smiled again and let the black man get on with his scrubbing. Tim cooked a large slice of bacon about as thick as a man's finger, then added some slices of baked potato and made some coffee. A bit later he took his grub to the bunkhouse and ate reflectively.

The sun was sinking below the horizon, streaking coloured fingers over the Yellow Hills as two men entered the bunkhouse, evidently finished with chores. One had been working with the smithy, judging from his sooty appearance. They nodded to Tim Hara, curtly, as men do who are unsure of each other.

Tim Hara wanted no confidants.

Unless, of course, he could use a man to discover the secret of Lander's Kingdom . . .

Three hours later there was silence in the bunkhouse, broken only by snores. The card games had finished. Men had washed in the cold water, cleaned their boots and beaten the dust out of their pants. All were asleep except the men out on guard. The night hung silent and moonless over the hills. Somewhere beyond the fortress a lone coyote howled.

Tim's moccasins were ready at the base of his bunk. His guns hung nearby. He lay under the single blanket, still wearing his shirt. His pants were ready to slip into.

He was tired, in a sense, from the early morning's work, but that feeling could be put aside.

Time was being wasted, he felt. He'd had to go along with the rustling exploit, which was a diversion that had produced no result so far as his mission was concerned. He had to discover one truth about Dane Lander and the rest would follow.

When he thought there would be no chance of detection from a returning guard, he slipped out of the bunkhouse. Keeping to the shadows, he made his way across to the silent house that had its rear in the sandstone caves. He soon found the side door. Now that he knew how to raise the inside catch, it was the work of moments with his knife to open the door.

He sidled down the dark passage and reached the place where the smooth rock walls indicated he was inside the cliff face. He still retained the iron key which opened the grille deep in the passages, but there was the problem of the heavy door that barred access to the prisoner. Somehow he had to see this woman, learn her identity, try to talk to her. Why was she locked away?

He had to be sure of certain facts before there could be any gunplay against Lander. He had hunches but he wanted facts. This prisoner was Lander's grim secret. Few of the gunmen who rode for him knew about this dark side of his life in this fortress — that much Tim Hara was certain about.

He came to the first lantern glowing eerily on the rocky ledge and he paused. He hefted his gun in the holster. He had brought only one Colt, leaving the other weapon behind, under his bunkhouse pillow. And he had his knife. But he hoped he wouldn't have to use gun or knife.

Maybe he would check some other tunnel before approaching the heavy wooden door. There might be some other way into the cave that housed this poor, mysterious prisoner. Or maybe he could find some metal that could be used as a crowbar on the door.

He recognised the tunnel that led to the room imprisoning the unknown woman, but there was another low-roofed passage that angled off to the left. Using his knife, he scratched an identifying mark on the rock-face and then went cautiously along this unknown passageway, hoping he'd encounter another lantern before the faint light faded altogether.

He thought he'd moved only about fifty yards into the crooked, subterranean way when he heard the sound of boots somewhere behind him.

Another servant carrying food? Or was it Lander?

He was glad that this tunnel had many nooks and angles. A man could press into a dark corner and remain unseen unless a light searched him out.

He listened to the footsteps. Boots, he decided, slowly and carefully moving towards him, treading lightly like a man stalking. Somewhere behind him the tunnel's darkness hid the man. The fact that he was creeping along meant that he was aware of the intruder.

Tim Hara found a recess in the cave wall and waited, his gun palmed. The sounds of the approaching man continued, now louder. A few more seconds of waiting and Tim changed his mind about the gun. The palming had been instinctive. He slid out his knife. The stealthy scuffing sounds came nearer and he could hear the man's breathing. There was still no shape, no outline in the darkness.

Then a match flared, casting a yellow, flickering light that moved erratically as the man took a few steps.

He was about seven yards from Tim. The match flame cast strange shadows on the angles and contours of the tunnel rock, and Tim knew he was just beyond the fringe of light.

Then he saw Dirk Schulman, bulky, hatless, a clumsy figure in the confines of this subterranean way.

8

Trickery

Janet Lander faced her father in the huge main room of the house.

'I want to see John Hertzog — tomorrow — and I won't take no for an answer!'

Lander had been countering her arguments for at least thirty minutes and he was incensed, although he kept a rein on his temper. It was late and he wanted to retire to the big old four-poster bed where he slept alone night after night. He had tried to gauge Janet's feelings for the young rancher, but she had been indefinite.

'You know I'll have to decide on which man to send with you if you insist on visiting the Palermo area . . . '

'Send anyone, Dad, but I must see John!'

'Do you have any affection for him?' He had asked that question twice before in different ways.

'I just want to see him,' she evaded. 'He — he's a nice young man and — '

'And you are a young girl with a driving need to find a husband — is that it?'

Her eyes flashed. 'I don't look at every man as a possible suitor! But, perhaps, in a way, you're right.' She suddenly brought her hands to her head. 'Oh, Dad, will you ever leave this place? Why can't we go away?'

'This is my world.'

'Do you want to die an outlaw?'

He turned from the huge stone fireplace where Indian carvings in wood and a fine hand-drawn map of the county decorated the chimney. In cord trousers, a dark blue shirt and a deerskin vest, Lander looked an imposing man. He thrust a hand through his thick grey hair and said grimly, 'I want you to be happy, Janet. Remember that, always! You can stay here or you can go to your aunt in Abilene. It's your choice.'

'For the moment I'll stay here. I want to persuade you to give up this lawless life and — '

'The moment I ride out of this place alone, the law will do its damnedest to ride me down,' he said.

'You're a prisoner here — afraid to leave!'

He couldn't meet her eyes. He strode to a heavy mahogany table, took the top off a round jar full of tobacco, found some papers and began to roll a smoke. The word 'prisoner' caused bitter thoughts to flood his mind, and his fingers were clumsy with the makings. He was a long time rolling the cigarette, and she watched him closely.

'Dad, you seem so worried. I'm sorry if I've said some unpleasant things.'

'You shouldn't have to apologise for speaking the truth.' He paced to the other side of the room. 'In a way you're right — I will die as an outlaw.' He laughed grimly. 'Life can be strange,

Janet. There were times when I had great respect for law, but I was young then.'

'When I was born?'

'About that time . . . '

'Tell me more. Tell me about my mother.'

'She's dead!' he said sharply.

'You've said that so many times, but I'd like to know more. Where is she buried? I — I'd like to put some flowers on her grave and — and just stand there.'

'That's impossible.'

'Why? You never explain.'

'Her grave is unmarked. There's nothing to see.'

'Can't you give me a picture of her?'

'There are none.'

A perplexed frown appeared on Janet's brow. 'It's so strange — as if you wanted to forget her.'

'Janet, please don't mention this subject again.' He dragged in smoke from his cigarette and felt he had to enlarge on what he'd said. 'Death is final, the end. When a person dies, he ceases to exist — it's almost as if he never existed! At least, that's the way it is with me.'

'But we're human and we have memories,' she said. 'God gave us the ability to remember people we've loved.'

His temper exploded. 'Will you stop? I don't want to be plagued by this fool talk! I don't want to remember!' He threw the cigarette butt into the fireplace. 'I'm going to bed. You can ride out tomorrow to see this young man at the Hertzog ranch. I'll arrange for someone to ride along with you.'

Helplessly, close to tears, she watched her father stride from the room. Once again an attempt to get him to talk about his early life had failed. He was adamant in his refusal to leave the place. He'd made it clear that his fate was bound up in this rocky hideout.

Her mind flashed back to her earliest childhood memories; the happy image of a woman . . . in a garden . . . in a large room. Then there were her years with the aunt in Abilene . . . infrequent meetings with the tall stranger who was her father . . . days at school in Abilene. There wasn't much that was coherent or had continuity.

She would ride out tomorrow and see John. He was so nice, so young and free from care. She liked him a lot, and of course, being a woman, she knew how he felt about her. Did she reciprocate this feeling? On this point she wasn't sure; there was the strange feeling in her breast when she thought of the lean, dark-eyed man who'd kissed her.

At about the same time Dane Lander broke off his conversation with his daughter, Tim Hara waited in the dark recess for the approaching figure of Dirk Schulman. The match burned out and with a curse Schulman threw it away. He moved another few steps, stopped and then struck another match. With the aid of the reddish-yellow light he stepped out again.

Without the light he might have

passed the concealed Tim Hara, but the match was flaring strongly.

Their eyes met — Tim's narrowed gaze, against the surprised, beady look of the fat man. Tim stepped forward lithely, his knife glinting. The point sliced straight at Dirk Schulman's big belly and stopped, making only a little incision in the tightly stretched shirt.

'Looking for me, partner?' Tim's mind was tuned to act on the man's reaction.

Lander's right-hand man stiffened. He stared down at the knife, then the match burned his fingers and he dropped it. In the darkness only the physical presence of the two men and the point of the knife made for reality.

'You found me, *amigo*,' Tim said in a whisper.

'I saw you, Hara — saw you mosey across from the bunkhouse. I wasn't asleep in my quarters.'

'You were watching, huh?'

'I was watching. Saw you open that side door.'

Tim laughed. 'Go ahead. You got more to say?'

'What in hell are you snoopin' around for, Hara? Why're you poking around in these passages?'

In the darkness only words carried significance. The knife was still a threat. A sharp thrust and blood would spurt and death would rush in with agonizing speed. It was a strange situation. In the blackness of the tunnel the tenseness that had built up was a tangible thing.

'You want answers, huh?' Tim parried. 'Well, I just got curious, feller. Queer house, ain't it? I just figured there were tunnels behind it so I came to see. You know, I'm always gettin' into grief with this urge of mine to poke my nose into the unknown.'

'That ain't no real answer, Hara, and you know it.' Dirk Schulman seemed to gain confidence. 'Put that knife away and we'll have a parley. I've got things to say.'

But Tim held the knife firmly against the ample belly. 'You got a gun?' He felt around the man's gunbelt with his free hand, located the single Colt and plucked it from its holster. He rammed it under his belt. 'All right, Dirk, now we can talk. Just remember that I'll kill you if I figure that you plan to trick me.'

Dirk Schulman said, 'Look, Hara, you think I'm Lander's man. Wal, that sure is right — but only up to a point. After that I'm my own boss. Do you follow me? I work for Lander, sure, but somewhere along the trail I figure to look after myself.'

'You trying to tell me something?'

'I know why you're nosin' around these tunnels — you figure Lander has his gold and some money stashed away back of the house. You've got all the gall in the world, Hara — I hand you that. You're the only cuss in this outfit who'd figure to cross Lander — except me.'

'You'd cross him? You'd tangle with Lander?'

'If there's a stack of dinero at the end of it. Lander buys only part of me. I ride and shoot for him. I knock these damned rannigans into shape, bawl them out, see they got horses, grub and water. I've been ramroddin' for Lander so long I forget when we first met. But who has all the money stashed away? Lander! I ain't got a damned dollar.'

'You've been paid.'

'Sure. But what the hell! A man gets to gambling a night in Famoso — and what happens? Skinned. Or a woman — there was one in Skaggs. Hell, I got nothin'. But Lander has real dinero stashed away — right here somewhere.'

'I know that.'

'Money, Hara — money! He's got it — and me, the fool who's prodded these damned gunslicks for years, what have I got?'

'You're bitter, huh? I didn't guess, Dirk. You cover up pretty well.'

'I don't show my hand. Ever.'

'You have — to me.'

'Yeah, but I got you dead to rights, Hara. I've been tryin' to figure you out . . . '

'I guessed that.'

'And now I know.' Dirk Schulman gave a little laugh. It was the most humourless sound Tim had ever heard. He said, 'You're a hellion, Hara. You've got guts. You don't pack them two guns just for show. All right, now I've put my cards on the deck. How about you?'

Tim had to make a decision. It was either go along with Dirk Schulman or kill the man right there.

Killing Schulman would create problems for Tim. What would he do with the body? Lander was no fool; he'd make guesses. No. Killing the hefty man wasn't something he could get away with.

'We have things in common,' Tim said. 'I'm after dinero, too. What else? But do you know where Lander has the stuff stashed? Where do all these tunnels lead to?'

'I don't know. That's it. I ain't ever been in these tunnels afore, but I knew there were caves behind the house.'

'That's easy to figure.'

'Sure. Most of the rannigans know

that. But nobody gets around the back of the house. So I guess that's where he stashes his gold and money.'

'Could be.' Tim eased back the knife. He wasn't really interested in Lander's wealth. His line of investigation had been well-defined. Probe into Lander's Kingdom, he had been told, and discover if there is any truth in the account one dying man had brought back to Fort Worth. Well, he had ascertained that there was a prisoner — a woman, at that — which supported the information he'd been given. But there was still the question of identity.

He knew that Dirk Schulman wouldn't be interested in anything but cash and gold. The fat man wouldn't cross Lander for anything else.

Tim didn't want Dirk Schulman as an accomplice, but it seemed he was stuck with him for the moment. He sighed and said, 'All right, Dirk. You and me — we'll make a play for Lander's cache. For a start, he's got my gold. But we can't do it tonight.'

'Why not?' There was an edginess to the rasping voice.

'Think, man. We need plans. We need horses stashed somewhere in a gully among the approach trails to this place. We need water, grub and maybe a packhorse or two. We might even need another hand.'

'No! Just you and me, Hara. We can handle it.'

Tim smiled in the dark. 'You figure a two-way split is the limit, eh? All right — but we need to plan this. A good idea would be to get the other hands away on some job — miles away — and you could fix that. Then we tackle Lander and get the dinero with no interruptions from some owlhoot who thinks he'll side with the boss. We need daylight for a job like this, and if the other galoots are pounding dust miles away — well, that would be fine. Do you get the picture, Dirk?'

Schulman's chuckle sounded in the gloom. 'Hell, you make it sound easy. Sure, that's the way. I can arrange some chore for most of the men, and I can even get Lander to swallow it.'

'Right. But we can't do anything tonight. All right, Dirk, we're partners — let's sleep on it.'

It was the only way out, Tim Hara thought. One thing was for sure; he was a loner and he had a job to do that he'd promised to see through. It was one way of earning remission for his earlier hellion days. Having Schulman as a sidekick wasn't in his plans, and Lander's money was something that should go back to its rightful owners when the Kingdom fell to attacking lawmen. That and only that was the real plan.

They walked to the side door of the house and slipped out, then they crept away singly, keeping to the shadows.

But fate came into play early the next day. Dirk Schulman sought out Tim Hara just after breakfast in the bunkhouse, when the men were astir seeing to their horses and other chores.

'Lander has a job for you,' Schulman

said. 'Wouldn't go for anythin' I said about sending another man. He wants you to ride out with his daughter to the Hertzog ranch.'

Tim stopped polishing his boots and looked up. 'Damn! Why me?'

'Reckon that's a good question,' Schulman sneered. 'He didn't see you kissin' the girl like I did!'

Tim laughed softly. 'You sure use those eyes of yours, Dirk. Just forget what you saw.' There was insistence in his low voice. 'Anyhow, it ain't what you think.'

Dirk Schulman looked around warily as he and Tim walked to the top of the bunkhouse steps. 'Sure, sure. It ain't my grief what you get up to with that girl. Just watch it, that's all. Lander once had a feller thrashed to near skin and bones because he tried to do what you done!'

'Forget it!' Tim's forefinger stabbed the other's chest.

'Sure, sure.' Dirk Schulman's big belly bumped against Tim's side. Tim pushed him back with splayed fingers on his chest. He disliked this fat renegade.

'What else?' he demanded.

'Lander wants to see you right away about this ride out with the girl.' Dirk crowded in again, confidingly. 'Have you figured out a plan?'

'Nope. I just got out of a warm bunk.'

'The blasted ride to that ranch will waste another day.'

Tim nodded, considering his own plans. Schulman was an obstacle. The ride out with the girl would keep him from seeing the prisoner in the cave, but there was always the night, without the ponderous Dirk.

He had to play the man along. 'Don't worry about a thing. Just start thinking of ways to trick the big man. Just think you could be rich pretty soon.' Tim smiled narrowly. He wondered who was the trickiest customer — himself, Schulman or Lander? Schulman was a snake, that much was clear now. 'You know this land better'n me,' Tim said, 'figure out ways of gettin' clear with packhorses in a hurry. Anything that might be useful. I guess I'd better get along to see Lander.'

'That's for sure. He don't like to be kept waitin'. You'd think this was the army the way he chucks out his orders.'

Only minutes later Tim Hara walked calmly up to the main door of the big house. Some attempt had been made to build a Spanish-style arch over the entrance. The black hinges bolted into the thick door gave it the appearance of a citadel. A lot of force would be needed to break down the door. He glanced around. The ground-floor windows had shutters which were equally as strong. It was just idle thinking, certainly, but if determined men — lawmen or others — were trying to break in, the occupants would have a lot of time to make an escape. Maybe the tunnels at the back of the rambling house provided for such an escape route. It was a possibility.

Dane Lander and Janet were waiting for him in the large square room. The servant who showed Tim Hara in just seemed to melt away. Lander smiled, a display of his old courtesy which he did not waste on his other hirelings, but was probably put on now for Janet's benefit.

'So Schulman gave you my message.'

'You want me to ride out with Miss Janet?'

'She's determined to see that young man, John Hertzog. Maybe it's a good idea. I agree she should have a change of surroundings, even see someone outside of this — this — ' Dane Lander groped for a word.

'This rocky jail,' suggested Tim.

He received a deep frown for his boldness. 'This place serves to shelter the likes of you, Hara. Remember that.' The frown faded. 'I liked your work with the rustling. But that was small stuff, you'll get something worthwhile before long. In the meantime, ride along with my daughter. If she wants to stop at the Hertzog ranch — and I know they have a reputation for hospitality — just stick around. Maybe that young ranny, John Hertzog, will have enough savvy to see that she gets back here safely. If he can't do that chore, you have the responsibility. Got that, Hara?'

'You trust me? What if I figured to ride off?'

'We've got your gold — and, you've earned a bonus already for the time you've been here. You won't ride.'

'Yeah, you got me to rights,' said Tim. 'I'll be back.'

Lander couldn't possibly guess at the real reasons why he'd be back. The secret of the Kingdom was still to be resolved.

Janet Lander flicked a cool glance over the lean, dark man who stood confidently before her. She noted the clean hands, the dark hair brushed back in a wave. He smelled of the antiseptic soap used in the bunkhouse. He was clean-shaven, something she liked. His firm lips curled smilingly and she was sure there were secrets behind the smile. With a man like Tim Hara there would be secrets. She knew nothing about him except that he carried two guns and had come up out of the trails. She had answered his kiss daringly because she was that kind of girl. And she had discovered one more thing.

He wasn't a scoundrel. It was a crazy, conclusion but she knew it to be true. There was the stolen gold and a wanted hand-bill on her father's desk — but there were other things which she knew instinctively.

They rode out while the morning sun was still low enough to allow fast cantering with the horses. The Yellow Hills receded until they were a smudge on the horizon.

During a spell when they allowed the animals to plod on, she began to talk:

'Do you like working for my father?'

'So far.'

'Yesterday you tried to convince me that he'd die an outlaw.'

'It sure seems like it.'

'I'd like you to know that I've tried to get him to leave the Yellow Hills, but he won't. He seems to have a strange affection for the place.'

'Maybe his fate is bound up with the fortress. A man can get that way — sometimes about a ranch, or a mine.'

'Yes. It is odd.'

'Maybe there are things he can't leave behind?'

'It's only a hideout — a house — rocks — heat — hard men!'

'Yeah, but those things are roots to some men, Janet.'

She smiled softly and pushed back her new fawn stetson. The cord was firm against a smooth, tanned little chin and her blonde hair was tucked into the hat and not hanging so bewitchingly down her neck as it usually did. She sat the saddle of the wiry mustang with assurance. There was no modesty about the way her long thighs curved over the animal's ribcage. She wore her jeans and a tightly buttoned blouse. He was well aware of her feminine charms, and once again it hit him, this knowing that she was all woman. Still, she was young and he had too many years of hard living behind him to even think like a fool youth who sees a pretty face for the first time. And she was riding out to see John Hertzog.

Unexpectedly, as if she had read his mind, she said, 'I like John. He's very nice.'

'Bein' nice is pretty important, ain't it?'

She flashed her eyes and laughed. 'Oh, dear! Is that bitterness I detect?'

'Could be. I'm not nice at all.'

'No.' She leaned forward and patted the mustang's mane. 'You're a hard man — but a good one!'

'Good? Listen, Janet, I've robbed and killed and — '

'So have other men — and repented. This land is full of men who lived by the gun and then became respected — lawmen, ranchers, stage operators.'

He nodded. 'I've met some. One

galoot, Harry Smith, was as fast as blazes with a rifle — used it like a Colt. Well, Harry settled down and became a sheriff — and then a preacher no less at Wichita Falls!'

'Well, you could do the same.'

'Settle down? You mean a wife, a home, kids?'

Her face flushed. 'Why not?'

He suddenly twisted in his saddle and stared along the trail. A moment later he heeled his roan up a shale slope, leaving Janet in the defile. She saw him shade his eyes, stand high in the stirrups and stare back along the route they had travelled. Then he rode quickly back to her.

'What was that for?' she asked.

'Thought I saw some trail dust.'

'Did you?'

'Nope. Some heat mirage, I reckon. Talkin' of heat, maybe we should give the horses some water.'

But he'd lied, suddenly deciding not to tell her that they were being followed. He'd seen the distant black shape of a rider against the red rock buttes. Someone was keeping a safe distance behind them. Maybe he thought he was too far back for anyone to see him, but he'd reckoned without the superb eyesight of one man. Who was the rider? A stranger? Or had Lander sent him?

9

Threats From A Stranger

They wasted some time in watering the animals, and this was what Tim Hara wanted. He poured water from his canteen into his hand and allowed the roan to suck it up. Then, slowly, he gave it more. With two water bottles on the saddle-horn, they had enough of the precious liquid for the comparatively short journey to the Hertzog ranch.

'This is sure some country,' he said casually to the girl. 'Men came here from across the sea and what did they find? Injuns, grass, gold — and a land too hot in summer and too cold in winter.' He recorked the bottle. 'Ever think of goin' east, Janet — to Virginy — and stare at the ships with the tall masts that sail in across Chesapeake Bay. Cool winds, Janet — with the tang of the sea. Seems a heck of a lot different to this place . . . '

Holding the reins of her pony, Janet moved closer to him. 'What are you trying to do?'

'Does that mean somethin'?'

'Why are you wasting time?'

'Didn't know I was. Just figured to talk some, Janet.'

'I really want to see John . . . '

'Sure, you do, Janet, and I'm the *hombre* to take you there.' He placed a gloved hand on her arm. She looked down. He saw her red lips, the full womanly hint that here could lie passion and generosity. As though feeling his eyes on her, she looked up.

'Mr. Hara, I allowed you to kiss me once, but . . . '

'But what, Janet?'

'You're a man of secrets and I'm not sure of you.' The shallow defile between the varicoloured rocks, now warm as an oven with the sun directly overhead, concealed them from the trail that led across the wide depression between the hills. The Hertzog ranch, with Palermo beyond it, was still some thirty miles distant, in the area where scrub mesquite and chaparral gave way to the bunch grasses so necessary for cattle.

He vaulted lithely to his saddle. 'Just stick around here, Miss Lander. Don't move away. I'll be back.'

'Where on earth are you going?'

He grinned. 'Privacy, young lady. We've been ridin' for some time . . . '

He saw her widened eyes, then he jigged the roan out of the dip and laughed quietly at her horrified reaction.

He sent his horse into a fast canter, down the shale slope, past some chaparral clumps, through a gap between boulders as high as a colonial-style house. He halted the horse in the scant shade of a rocky overhang. He could see the distant rider; he was nearer than before, almost within identifying range. The man was reading their trail-marks; giving his attention to the ground immediately in front of him.

As he waited, Tim wondered if the man was one of Lander's gunslicks. There was always a chance that Lander would use trickery in even the straightest of deals. As the rider came on, pushing his dust-coated nag to a trot, Tim failed to recognize him as one of the men he had seen in the Kingdom. He had made it a definite policy to get a good look at most of the *hombres* who rode for Lander, realizing that there could be men he had missed.

Tim hugged the curve of the overhang and maintained his vigilance. The other's face was clearer now. Tim was sure the man hadn't come from the Yellow Hills hideout. For one thing, his horse was dead tired. He looked like he'd been riding for some days out in the badlands; the horse's leathers were caked with dust. Three water bottles jiggled from the saddle-horn.

Tim Hara thought of a direct approach. He could ride down and tell the rider to hit dust in another direction. He might discover why the gent was trailing them.

Tim jigged his roan into a fast canter that brought the animal in a hoof-clattering rush over loose rock and sand. The other man jerked up his head, reined in and froze. Tim Hara held his leathers with one hand and kept his right fist dangling loosely near the Colt butt.

The other rider was cast in the lean, unshaven, hawklike mould of the sun-wearied range man. He wore a black, flapping vest, a green cotton shirt. Scuffed chaps were laced over black pants and a white gunbutt curved clear of its holster. He carried saddle-bags and bedroll on his small horse.

'You've been readin' that track real good!' Tim flung the comment and then brought the roan to a halt, close enough to read the man's expression. The rider smiled.

'It's good to know there's someone else out here.'

'That all?'

'Yeah. I'm headin' for Palermo.'

'Are you lost?'

'What the hell d'you mean? No, I'm not lost.'

'Men do get lost in this land — if they get thirsty and suffer delusions.'

'I ain't lost.'

'You can start tellin' me the truth!' snapped Tim Hara. 'I know you've been trailin' us for some time — and you ain't lost, *amigo*. You're just plumb followin' us. Why?'

'I tell you — I figured to catch up, have a bit of a parley . . . '

'Where're you from?'

'I've been around . . . '

'Did you look in at Famoso?'

'Yeah. I didn't stop long.'

'Well, take another trail, *hombre*. I get nervous when some rannigan hangs on my heels!'

'Why, you damned owlhoot!' shouted the other man. 'You got gall, tellin' me what to do! I saw you a long ways off, *hombre* — with a telescope glass — and I know you. Hell, the sheriff came into Famoso with a posse lookin' for you!'

'Is that so?' Tim muttered.

There was a sudden drumming of hoofs, then Janet appeared between the boulders, riding hard. She dragged her mount up fast when within speaking distance of Tim. 'Why, Mr. Hara, I think you knew we had company . . . ' Unafraid, she looked at the travel-stained man. 'Who is this?'

'A galoot who's ridin' on!'

Temper seemed to be the stranger's weakness. He seemed unable to halt his angry retort. 'I ain't allowin' you to talk to me like that! The sheriff in Palermo would like to know where to lay his hands on you. Yeah. Should be some dinero in that for me. And that ain't all!'

'Ride on, you fool!' Tim said.

'I've brought in outlaws like you afore,' snarled the man. 'I've picked up bounties from Pecos to Brownwood — and I knew you from the minute I saw that wanted poster in the cantina at Famoso. Tim Hara — the hardcase from San Antonio way. You made a fool play when you picked up that gold from Palermo. Seems that big outlaw, Dane Lander, lifted it from you.'

'You know a lot.'

'It's a big desert but a small world of men, mister. A little lawyer feller spread the news in Famoso that you'd gone to work for the big man — and I was around to hear.' He pointed a finger. 'You're worth money dead or alive, Hara. I've been lookin' through the badlands for a sign of you for days now. Figured you might have the gold — and then I heard you'd moved in with the big owlhoot. Almost gave up. But here you are . . . with the girl, too. Lander's daughter, I reckon.'

'What do you figure that means, stranger?'

'I reckon you're on the way to Palermo for some reason. It don't matter what. And I ain't puzzling my head about the girl. All I know is that you're worth reward money, Hara. I'm ridin' on, like you want, but I ain't gonna be too far away.'

Tim gave a slow smile. 'It's a big country and I advise you to get lost in it. Just ride — and by the way, I ain't worried about the sheriff in Palermo. For one thing, we ain't headin' for that town.'

Bad temper still consumed the man. He said, 'You don't think I know much about you, do you? Well, I seen you long afore I saw that wanted bill in Famoso. Yeah! Seen you once in San Antone. You were gittin' on the stage for Fort Worth!'

Tim Hara stiffened. Sure, he had been to Fort Worth, after the meeting with Captain Morgan and the federal marshal from Sansemo. He'd been to see the top man, General Charlton, feeling that he wanted more information, and right from the man who counted. He'd gotten it.

'Sure figured a cuss with your rep would stay clear of the army!' the stranger said.

'I've got friends in Fort Worth,' Tim said.

'Queer. Ain't a place for a known two-gun man . . . '

'Ride!' There was so much vehemence in Tim's rasping order that Janet Lander glanced at him in surprise.

'You tellin' me what to do again?' Sheer rage swept away all the stranger's caution. It was as if he had hated the man before him for a long time. Hatred and anger were a bad mixture in a land where guns spoke as fast as a challenging word.

'Ride away, stranger,' said Tim quietly. 'Don't prod!'

'I've been on the side of the law all my life!' the man shouted. 'I've picked up bounty money! I've tangled with the worst!' His eyes glinted insanely. Each word brought froth to his dust-laden lips as he built up a crazy fury against Tim Hara. 'I figure you're just a show-off, mister — a mean *hombre* on the run. You ain't foolin' me with them two hoglegs! You ain't used them much! Hell, you're a snake and them guns is just a front! I know you, Hara! You're

147

wanted — a walkin' dead man! You was snoopin' around the army at Fort Worth for somethin — I was told that later by a feller who travelled with you! I don't like you and you don't fool me!'

Maybe the heat and loneliness of the man's solitary ride had fanned his bitter nature to the point where he could hardly reason. Whatever the cause, there was no time for analysis in the next few grim moments. Tim Hara guessed it was coming, and he wished to God it was not to be, but when the man's hand suddenly flashed to his gunbutt all the instincts of self-preservation stabbed him into action.

Years of gun drill had given him a speed with the draw that couldn't be halted once the signal had activated his brain.

His two hands moved as one. Two hands, two guns — and it wasn't for flashy display. The stranger, pushed on by his mad hatred, had his long-barrelled Colt clear of leather quickly — but he wasn't fast enough.

Three guns roared and startled the horses into a frantic prancing. The slug from the desert man's Colt whipped through the air far above Tim Hara's head as the man was slammed back by the two guns.

The man dropped his gun, slowly, his face contorted, eyes staring. He began to topple slowly from his saddle as agony tore through his body. The two slugs had drilled him above the heart. As he slid like a weighted sack to the dust, his foot jerked in a stirrup and the horse wheeled, taking the body around in a ground-scraping circle.

Tim Hara slowly replaced the guns. The old grim tingle slid down his spine and he swallowed hard, pushing back the tautness of his throat muscles.

The stranger's horse steadied, ears pricked back, eyes wide with fear. The lifeless bundle, still hooked by one leg to the stirrup, poured red blood into the dusty earth.

Tim Hara glanced at the girl. He just had to see her expression, her reaction.

That she was afraid was to be expected. That she should stare at him in horror was something he hadn't considered. He had tangled with fast gunhands before and left them dead and had ridden away in a mood of finality. That was all.

But a lithe, blonde girl of medium height had not been around to look at him.

He met her gaze. 'He asked for it — the fool! You saw him prod me. He wanted to kill me.' He flicked a disgusted glance at the body. 'Why the devil didn't he ride away? I told him to get!'

'You've killed a man,' she said slowly. 'It's so horrible! Couldn't you have shot the gun out of his hand or — or wounded him?'

'I shoot to kill.' The admission was tight-lipped.

'Was there no other way?'

'Janet, I react in only one way.'

'To kill?'

He tapped the holsters, a bitter twist

to his lips. 'These guns have kept me alive. I can use them only one way. They have to be fast, certain. There's no room for tricks.'

She turned her horse. The animal's nostrils flared at the scent of blood and she said:

'Oh, God, let's get away from here! Let me get to the Hertzog ranch where I can see John.'

'Yeah, he's from a real nice family,' Tim said dryly.

'There's peace and beauty at that ranch!'

'I reckon there is. Did you know that old man Hertzog wiped out a band of Indians one night just because they got drunk on white man's whisky and wanted to walk around his walls? If they'd been white, it would've been funny and taken as that. But they were Injuns, so his men shot and killed the lot. Not a word was raised in Palermo. Sure, it's a nice place.'

'You have a horrible sense of humour!'

'Yeah. Like you said, Janet, I'm not nice.'

'I want to move out of here!' she said. 'Will you get started and — and — bury that man? If you don't hurry, I'll ride on alone.'

'You sound just like your pa,' he drawled. 'You got the same way of givin' orders.'

'And you?' She was stung into retaliation. 'What are you? And why did this man think there was something strange about you being seen in Fort Worth?'

'One place is the same as another . . . '

'That's not true. Fort Worth is the last place a wanted man would visit. I'm not a fool, Tim Hara. I've heard about Fort Worth. These days it's the most law-abiding town any one could find, what with the army and town marshal and the federal courts all situated there. What were you doing in Fort Worth?'

'Like I said, I have friends there.'

'You don't convince me,' she said,

suddenly thoughtful, her flawless face set hard. 'I can see you're lying. Yes, Tim Hara, I know when you're lying!'

He got down from the roan and pulled the dead man's foot free of the stirrup. He dragged the body to a rocky patch of ground; made a depression by moving some small rocks and then he placed the body in it. He spent fifteen long minutes heaping rocks over the corpse, making a rough cairn.

He returned to Janet reading a small notebook he'd taken from the man's vest pocket. 'Name of Cheyney. Fred Septimus Cheyney. Seems he has some relatives in San Antonio. A brother. Maybe I'll write and let him know.'

'Oh, that's terribly good of you!' she said sarcastically. He got aboard and threw a cold smile at her.

'You seem to have taken a dislike to me.'

'You're right — I can't like you at the moment.' She shook her head help-lessly. 'I'm not sure of you. Who are you?'

'Tim Hara, at your service. Let's go. You want to see John Hertzog and I've got orders to get you there. That's all there is between us, Janet.'

They rode on in silence. Where there had been trust, now there was tension.

He was perturbed, not because she had seen him kill a man and was upset, but because he was afraid she'd make some shrewd guesses about his visit to Fort Worth. Or, if she mentioned it to her father, his wary mind would work on the few facts. The girl had heard a few unrelated comments from the man called Cheyney, but the details about Fort Worth were damning. No man with a wanted poster circulating around the frontier towns would go anywhere near Fort Worth. The place was thick with lawmen and the army.

They rode on through the day and stopped once for a meal. It was water and cold beans eaten with a spoon from the can. Hardly a grand meal but it would sustain them.

She barely spoke to him. She had

been shocked by the violent way the man had died. She had seen a side of Tim Hara which dismayed her. As for Tim, he was beginning to think it was better that she should look at him this way. Maybe now she'd give John Hertzog her favours. He had other things to do.

10

Visit To Palermo

The Hertzog ranch was not the biggest in the Palermo region but the stock and buildings were good and there was an air of prosperity about the Spanish-style ranchhouse. They rode through the gates and past the pole corrals, where they heard the shouting of men as mustangs were broken. Somewhere a blacksmith was using a hammer on an anvil. Away in the distance blue hills rose behind the town of Palermo. Tim wondered how Sheriff Luke Dugald was faring.

Dent Hertzog, John's father, was a silver-haired man of dignity and shrewdness. Slight, wiry, hook-nosed, he wore a store suit, although the day was too warm for anything heavier than pants and a shirt. His manner was polite, inquiring, almost European. But he was second generation American; he'd sided with the Confederates and had survived the defeat to become a wealthy man.

He knew that Tim Hara was probably wanted by the law, but he treated him as a guest. 'You're most welcome, Mr. Hara.' In a way his attitude was dictated by the way John had enthused over Janet's visit.

John Hertzog had been out with the men and his shirt and pants were soiled with work stains. He was hardly the immaculate young range man that Tim had originally seen. But Janet greeted him with warmth, and John's young face lit up with delight. 'It's good to see you, Janet!'

'And good to see you, John! You look fit! I gather you didn't encounter any more Mescaleros on your ride back here.'

'Just a boring ride!' He laughed and glanced at Tim Hara. 'I never got the chance to thank you for the way you helped when Lander tried to ride his horse over me.'

'Think nothing of it.'

'He's a hard man.' John shoved his hat back on his head and looked down at his dirty hands. 'Heck, I'll have to clean up, Janet, now that you're here.' He glanced at his father. 'I'll want some time off, Dad. I can make it up later.'

'Sure — and escort Miss Lander inside. She must be tired after her long ride. Ask Mrs. Pinder to prepare the guest room for Miss Lander. I'll see the cook — we must have a worthy meal for our guests.'

'This is a great day!' John Hertzog lightly held the girl's arm. Tim Hara noted the intimate touch and kept a poker face. John went on: 'You must stay for a few days, Janet. Mrs. Pinder, the housekeeper, will see to your comfort and I'll show you around the ranch.'

'I'd like that.'

Tim stepped up to Hertzog. 'Look, if you'll ride back with Miss Lander to the Yellow Hills, I'll be able to head back right now. If you can't take off enough time for that, I'll stick around and see her back whenever she wants to go. That was my order.'

'Of course I'll ride back with Janet,' John said. He was unsure of Tim Hara; the flicker in his eyes proved it.

'Fine,' Tim said. 'I guess I'll head back, if you'll let me wash up and take care of the horse.'

'You mean you'll leave right away? That's a hard trail.'

'Maybe, but that's the way I want it. I'll ride out before sundown.'

But Tim Hara had no intention of riding back to the Yellow Hills on an owlhoot trail. He would head for Palermo and Sheriff Luke Dugald. This trip to the Hertzog ranch was an ideal opportunity to make contact with the sheriff and give him a report on Lander's Kingdom. The sheriff could pass on the facts to others who were vitally concerned with Dane Lander.

Tim left the ranch about an hour

later, assuring Janet that he was taking a slow ride back to the Yellow Hills. There was an element of risk here, for the girl might casually mention the time of his departure to her father when she returned to the hideout. In that case he'd claim that he had made camp somewhere. Maybe she would just forget this detail. There were always imponderables; you had to keep thinking ahead.

It was dark when he saw the lights of Palermo. Moonlight lay gently on the downward trail into the town. He rode past clumps of cottonwood and redwood, and then encountered the first rough shacks. He smiled thinly as he recalled his first ride out of this town, with the gold bags on his saddlehorn.

The roan just walked along, head down; but Tim knew there was still speed left in the horse if a fast burst was needed. He didn't expect any trouble. He would enter the town quietly and leave the same way.

He rode to a hitching rail near the

bank where the shadows would hide his horse. It was quiet here, but down the main stem lights spilled from the saloons and Tim could hear the honky tonk tones of pianos.

Tim Hara patted the roan, then walked in the shadows until he reached the sheriff's office. He peered into the window, seeing faint light. Luck was with him. Luke Dugald was in his black oak chair, his feet on the desk. He was smoking his huge, evil-smelling pipe.

Tim knocked and walked in, grinning as Dugald swivelled in his chair and muttered a surprised oath.

'Good to see you,' Tim said.

'I'll be damned.' The portly sheriff smiled in admiration. 'In and out of that nest of vipers! Tim, I figure you got some talkin' to do!'

'Sure.' Tim sank into a chair. 'You still got that bottle hidden in the cupboard? I'm not much of a drinkin' man, but I reckon I could use a measure right now.'

'And you're mighty welcome.'

The first thing the sheriff attended to was the door. He slid the bolt shut and pulled down the blinds. He then went to his cupboard and got out the cherished bottle. It was always Colonel Grant's whisky with Luke Dugald; he wouldn't drink any other. He poured two large tots.

They were about to drink when loud banging came from a passage beyond the main office. It sounded like a man hitting a wooden object on iron bars.

'I got me a tearaway in the jail,' Luke grunted. 'Hold that drink a minute, Tim, while I tell him to stop his damned row. Blasted rowdy! He'd been creatin' a rumpus in the Black Ace Saloon, so I locked him up.'

The sheriff opened a door and sidled down the passage. Then he shouted, 'Shut your big mouth — and put that stool down or you'll be in the calaboose for a week!'

'I want out, Sheriff!'

'Well, makin' noise ain't the way to do it, feller.'

The door suddenly swung all the way open on its well-oiled hinges and Tim Hara found himself directly in the line of vision of the man behind the bars of the small cell. The man stared — hard. Too late, Tim swivelled his chair around. But the prisoner had taken a good long look.

'Say, Sheriff, you got yourself a rustler!' the prisoner announced. 'I saw that face afore! Took a good look at him the night I was ridin' herd on that bunch of cows that was rustled.'

'You're *loco*!' Luke said.

'I tell you he's one of the rannies who took off with that herd. I saw him sure as all hell! Him and his friends killed two of my buddies! I saw him!'

'You made a mistake,' Luke Dugald said.

'Listen, Sheriff, you've got to believe me — that's one of them murderin' rustlers!'

'I don't take the word of a tearaway. You've been drinkin' in town and raisin' hell — now you want to start

163

something else.'

The man gripped the iron bars. Tim Hara moved away to a corner of the office so the prisoner couldn't see him.

'What'n hell's he doin' in your office, anyway, Sheriff?'

'He's here on business . . . ' Luke Dugald moved back and closed the heavy door between the office to the cells. He turned to Tim. 'Tarnation!'

'It's nothing to worry about,' Tim said. 'I should've been more careful.'

'That damned door swings open too easy!'

They could hear the man still shouting on the other side of the wall.

'Anyway, Tim, your being here is just his word against mine,' Luke muttered. 'And he won't be out for a couple of days for his pesky cheek. You were in on that damned raid in the valley?'

'Yeah. Hand-picked by Lander. I didn't like the killin', Luke, but there was nothing I could do about it. I had to play it safe. Lander roughed me up a bit — had me thrown in his jail and took the gold. I had to act tough.'

'You are tough.'

'Maybe. Anyway, there's a chance the cattlemen can get that herd back. It's hidden in a secret box canyon near Halligan's ranch. Lander figures to sell that beef to miners on the Indian Territory.'

Luke nodded, then he said, 'How'd you get away to come here?'

'I had to ride with Janet Lander to the Hertzog ranch.'

'Why'd she go there?'

'Well, seems she's sweet on young John Hertzog.' Tim sipped at his drink and remembered how appealing Janet had looked. But he had to harden himself against such weaknesses. Shrugging, he began talking quickly, earnestly. 'I've been spyin' around that damned fort in the hills, Luke. Lander has a prisoner, a woman.'

'So that tale we were handed is true?'

'In a way. I haven't identified the woman yet.'

'But the crazy yarn must be right . . . '

'Hold it, Luke. I didn't actually see this woman.' Tim rammed one fist into the palm of his hand, emphasizing points. 'Sure, there's a woman — locked away — hidden in some cave at the back of Lander's big house. I heard some wild laughter — chattering — it was damned weird. I couldn't get past the door of her room.'

'She's locked away, eh? So that part of the story is true.'

'What else? It had to be a woman I heard. I saw light in a cave-like room, and then I saw somebody movin' around.'

Luke Dugald unlocked a drawer in his desk and took out a faded photograph. He stared at the picture of a pretty woman. 'As you say, Tim, you didn't see the person. But take another look at this picture. Refresh your memory.'

Tim frowned. 'What good is it? That picture was taken a long time ago. If she's the woman in Lander's place, then she must have changed a lot.'

'Yeah, that'd be right. So all you can report is that there is a woman held prisoner. We don't know why and we don't know for sure who she is.'

'Not for sure,' Tim agreed. He leaned forward. 'Listen and I'll tell you all about that damned hideout — the trails leadin' in — the men and the layout — and also what I intend to do. You can report back to Captain Morgan — and then I reckon he'll get in touch with General Charlton at Fort Worth.'

Tim filled in all the details with Luke Dugald, then they discussed the possible ways to deal with Lander.

'You know what the orders are,' Luke warned. 'The woman comes first. Okay — you've established that she's there. Now, if you could only get her out of that place.'

'And take Lander — dead or alive.' Tim nodded. 'It won't be easy . . . '

'Partner, I sure agree with that! But you're the only feller I know with the nerve and brains to do it.'

'I have a big incentive — my pardon,'

said Tim grimly. 'I'm the hellion who can do the impossible while the uniforms sit around in Fort Worth.'

Luke nodded. 'That's how it stands right now, son . . . '

Tim rode out of town the way he had entered, a dark figure hunched on a slow-moving horse. He was part of the night, an unknown rider. Tim took the well-defined trail west, skirting fences and groups of cattle bunched in grassy hollows. The roan moved on steadily, a willing animal with reserve of stamina available, but it was a fact that the horse had been overworked that day. Tim Hara knew he'd have to make camp somewhere. He didn't intend to ride non-stop to the Yellow Hills.

After the heat of day, the night was distinctly cool. He chose a grassy bank near some trees, just a few yards back from the trail. He loose-hitched the horse, took the saddle off and got out his bedroll.

Wrapped in the blankets, he suddenly realized he was dead tired. He'd had too much riding; first to the Hertzog place and then to Palermo, then along this trail. He dropped off, into a deep, untroubled sleep.

It was the solid, dreamless fatigue that overtakes a man whose energy has been sapped. The mysterious demands of body and brain take a man into the dark depths — the 'little death' that brings new strength. But not this time.

Rough hands seized him and heaved him up. He tried to struggle.

Three men held him and snarled accusations and abuse. One punched him in the stomach. Tim Hara buckled.

'Damned murderin' skunk!'

'It's him! Sure thing — it's him . . .'

'You're right, Jed. I'd recognise that big roan anywhere. What'll we do with him?'

'String him up!'

Tim Hara recovered from the punch in the stomach the slow way, dragging in air and spitting bile. The men held him fast.

'I don't hold with necktie parties,' said one.

'This hellion and his gang shot up two good men! I was there with that herd doin' nightwork. It was just after sunup and we were sittin' quiet in the saddle, with the beef nice and peaceable. And then up rides this murderin' bunch and they start shootin'. Them two men didn't have a chance, I tell you!'

Tim Hara got his first good look at the speaker. He saw the twisted, angry, snarling face. He was the trouble-maker who'd been in Luke Dugald's jail only two hours ago!

11

Hangnoose Brand

'Listen,' Tim Hara said, 'I didn't shoot any *hombre* riding on that herd that night.'

'How the hell do we know that? You were there.'

It was impossible to argue out of that. 'Take me back to the sheriff,' Tim said.

'Yeah? Seems to me that damn badge-toter and you are in cahoots!'

'How the blazes did you get out of jail?' Tim demanded angrily.

The cowpuncher laughed. 'I got pals, too.' Hard eyes in a craggy face glared at Tim Hara. 'My boss bought me out and the sheriff had to open up that cell. Then I collected my two pals. I had a hunch you'd be on this trail — it's the way out to the badlands.'

'Look, I can explain everything.' Tim swung to face the other two men. He saw accusing eyes. 'Look, fellers, let's go back to Palermo and see the sheriff. I won't try any tricks.'

'That you won't!' shouted the man known as Jed. 'You're gonna dangle! That's the way to deal with guntoters like you!'

'Now hold on, Jed,' said a man.

'Hell, are you with me or not? You were workin' that herd that night! Are you gettin' soft-livered? Why in hell should we bother takin' this hellion back to town? Especially when he's pals with the sheriff!'

'That's right.' One man agreed with Jed. He gripped Tim's arm with fresh force. 'I say get the rope ready. C'mon — we ain't got all night. The saloons are still open back in town. Let's get on with it and head back.'

Tim Hara struggled but two men held him fast. Jed walked back to where the three horses had been hitched to a dead tree. He returned swinging a coiled rope.

'Use his own horse,' Jed ordered. 'Tie his hands. Leave them hoglegs right where they are — might teach other gunnies a lesson if they see him danglin'.'

'It ain't right,' said the one dissenting man. 'We could ride back to town and let the law deal with him.'

'You forgotten our friends who were shot down?'

'No, but — '

Tim Hara felt the cold certainty that death leered at him only minutes away. His hands were tied and he was lifted onto his horse. Then the rope noose was around his neck. Jed whipped the other end of the rope over a tree branch, pulled it down and tied it firmly on a low branch.

'Let's get on with it!' Excitement held Jed. The power to reduce a living man to a corpse is a consuming emotion and Jed was gripped by it. He had justified everything in his mind and had argued the others into accepting the hangnoose as the solution. He was dealing out justice.

'Listen! Just get me to the sheriff!' Tim shouted. 'You've got things all wrong!' He jerked around to look at the one hesitant man. 'Don't let them do this!'

'I ain't so sure — ' the man began.

'You must know Luke Dugald is straight,' Tim said. 'Let him deal with this!'

'Get that damned horse moving!' Jed snarled. 'He's a two-gun snake if ever I saw one! Slap that horse!'

'This is lynch law!' Tim cried desperately.

'You bet, mister!' Jed strode over to the fidgety roan. His hand came down with a resounding thump on the horse's flank. The animal sprang forward with a shrill cry. Tim swung forward, boots scraping the animal's ribs, then he curved backwards in a slow arc.

The rope bit deep. Tim jerked, struggled. The three men gave the struggling figure one glance and then, as if by common assent, ran for their horses. They vaulted into the saddles and rode off. The roan veered in a circle and halted, afraid, kicking at the ground.

The three men galloped their horses hard along the trail into Palermo. Only one of them looked back, white-faced, afraid.

Sheer black depths welcomed Tim Hara after the first few moments of the choking, frightening knowledge that he was dying. The rope tightened, bit into flesh and muscles, cut blood vessels and skin.

*   *   *

The man who came back was terrified. Or was it a conscience that made him return? But he did come back and he wasted no time.

He cut the dangling man down. Tim's body fell lifelessly to the ground and lay like a black blotch on the grass.

The man sheathed his knife and glanced around fearfully. He turned the body over, curiously, not expecting any sign of life. He loosened the noose, pulled it free and then looked at the deep crimson bruise that ran like a brand around Tim Hara's neck. The man cursed, wishing to high heaven he'd been somewhere else when Jed had swaggered up.

Suddenly the man who should have been dead sucked for air. His mouth opened wide and a swollen tongue moved. Tim Hara made rasping sounds. The man went over to Tim's fallen saddle and got the water canteen.

In a few moments he was helping Tim to drink. Water trickled into Tim's mouth and onto the ground. Some minutes later the rangehand saw Tim's eyes open. The bright, uncomprehending stare of a semi-conscious man was too much for the rangehand.

'Listen — I didn't want to do this . . . '

But Tim Hara had not reached the point of understanding. He'd been floating in the black pit and the return to reason was something that took time. He swam back into a world where terrible visions danced in front of his eyes. His mouth and tongue were monstrous; he could hardly speak and his brain provided no coherent thought.

But the rangehand was there, compelled to administer to the man he had tried to hang. For some reason he couldn't ride away. Grimly, roughly, he gave Tim more water — and waited.

Tim's eyes cleared, focused, stared with some understanding. He attempted words.

'Thanks . . . mister . . . '

'What in hell am I gonna do with you?' muttered the rangehand.

There was no reply from Tim Hara. He was trying to swallow. He was breathing regularly. With returning awareness, the pain in his neck was excruciating. There was a weakness throughout his body that would need time to ease.

'Hertzog . . . ranch . . . ' he said raspingly.

'What — what — you tryin' to tell me something?'

'Get — my — horse.'

'Sure.'

'Get me to . . . Hertzog . . . place . . .'

'Listen, I've bucked Jed! He'll be mighty sore. Anyway, he was right — you were rustlin' stock!'

'Look, do the right thing — get me — to — Hertzog — you'll be — rewarded — just — see — that I get there.'

'All right. I'll get your nag and I'll see that you don't fall off on the way to the Hertzog spread. I know old man Hertzog — worked for him. I'll stick by anything he says.'

Tim Hara was able to sit up after some minutes. He stared at the cut rope and shuddered with his returning memories. He put a hand to his throat, felt the painful weal. Grimly, he realized he would carry the brand of the hangrope for a long time.

The other man retrieved the roan and saddled it. He got everything ready, then he helped Tim Hara up to the saddle.

They rode out, slowly. They went on and on, encountering no other man. It was a long, laborious ride. Tim nearly fell from the saddle as the roan mounted some rough ground, but willpower kept him hunched in the leather. The other man watched him curiously from time to time, wondering about this strange individual with the gunman's display of holsters and Colts, wondering about his own position as party to an attempted lynching.

The Hertzog ranch came into view, silent under the moon. Somewhere inside the large adobe wall that surrounded the place a dog began to bark, challenging the approach of the two riders.

When they rode into the courtyard, the dog's fierce barking brought men to the veranda. One was John Hertzog.

Tim Hara nearly fell into his arms.

'What's happened?' John glanced up at the rangehand.

The man drew a deep breath. 'I — I found him — hangin'. He was nearly gone. Says he knows you. Is that right?'

'Sure. He's Tim Hara.'

'Name don't mean anythin' to me.'

'Where did you find him?'

'On the trail — near a stand of trees.'

'He rode out of here some time ago.'

'Is that so? Wal, he's been in Palermo — talkin' to the sheriff. Leastways, that's what I was told.'

'The sheriff?' John Hertzog supported Tim and stared questioningly. Tim seemed too weak to talk. 'I just don't understand that, friend. This man wasn't headin' for Palermo when he left us.'

The ranchhand was uneasy. He was itching to go. He had done all that was humanly required of him, he thought. 'Well, it ain't no business of mine. But this *hombre* was in Palermo. Seems he knows Sheriff Luke Dugald. Well, I'm ridin' on, Mr. Hertzog. I done all I can.'

'Tim Hara knows the sheriff?' repeated John Hertzog. 'But that seems strange. He — '

The young rancher was about to say that Tim was an outlaw, a wanted man, a renegade who had just recently joined Dane Lander in his Yellow Hills roost, but he cut short his intended words.

'I'm goin',' said the rangehand. 'If you know so much about this *hombre*, maybe you can deal with him. *Adios*, Mr Hertzog. I'm gettin' the hell out of it!'

12

Ride Back — Alone

They kept him in bed in a room at the ranchhouse and fed him hot soup when he wakened after a restless night. He had tossed and turned and muttered in his sleep, unaware that John Hertzog was in his room.

John had been thoughtful as he watched the man heave and murmur in his sleep. The grim brand mark around his neck was now a deep red weal that would be with him for a long time.

For hours, Tim Hara watched the sun climb. He felt he could ride again despite his exhaustion — he had to ride. He told John Hertzog of his decision when the younger man entered the room with more food.

'You're not fit,' Hertzog said.

'A man can rest in the saddle.'

'Maybe.' John put the soup down on a table. 'Janet has agreed to be our guest for a few days,' he said slowly. 'My father is mighty pleased with her. If you insist on ridin', tell Lander that Janet should be out of that hellroost. Anythin' could happen to her in that lawless place.'

'Sure. I agree. But Janet sticks with her father because she figures she can persuade him to pack up that life.'

'He's a wanted man,' John said grimly. 'And so are you. Which brings me to a point, Hara. The man who brought you here last night said you'd been to see Sheriff Dugald. How come? You told us you were headin' for Yellow Hills.'

'What else did this man tell you?'

'Something about rustling. Were you in on that big raid on the herd rounded up in the valley?'

'Yeah — Lander got the cattle. I had to go along.'

'I don't get it. How does that square with you visitin' the sheriff?'

Tim Hara reached for his pants which were folded over a chair. 'Forget it, John. Thanks for the help. Just get me a steak and trimmings and then I'll ride. How's my horse?'

'He's as tough as you, Hara — and fed and watered.'

Tim saw Janet half an hour later, when he was eating in the dining hall of the big ranchhouse. She was wearing a gingham dress which she'd apparently borrowed. She looked fresh and lovely, utterly feminine. At that moment, with his throat still sore, the scar hidden by a clean bandanna, he had the chilling feeling that Janet belonged here at the Hertzog ranch. She seemed far out of the reach of a man who owned only a horse, saddle and guns.

'Howdy, Janet. You look real good.'

She was concerned about him. 'You should rest. John tells me you're riding out.'

'Yeah — back to the hills.'

'Why?' she challenged. 'Why, Tim Hara? To kill and rob?' She studied his

184

face, her eyes puzzled. 'Last night you went to see the sheriff. Why didn't he lock you up? Somehow I connect your visit to the sheriff with your trip to Fort Worth!'

He was finished eating. He got up from the table and stretched aching muscles that he knew would relax after an hour or two in the saddle. He said, 'That feller was wrong about me and Fort Worth. Anyway, Janet, you're too lovely — too young — to worry about dirt and death. Stay here at this ranch and — and — '

'And what?'

'Get married — to John!' he blurted out.

Soon he was at the saddled roan, adjusting the leathers. He glanced up as John Hertzog approached him.

'I hoped to speak to you afore I rode out.' Tim paused. 'I want you to do something — and don't ask fool questions. Just leave for Palermo and see Luke Dugald. Tell him to get some good gunhands — men who want to get rid of Dane Lander bad enough to risk lead. Tell him to make camp some miles out of the Yellow Hills. Tell him to stay in a gully out of sight of Lander's spies; as he's got 'em spread around like an army that'll be some chore. Within twenty-four hours of their makin' camp, they'll see a smoke signal — Injun-style. When they see it, they've got to ride in along the gullies that lead to that fort.'

'From all I know about that place, an invading posse will die in those gullies,' said John, narrow-eyed.

'Not this time,' said Tim Hara. 'You got all that? Repeat it.'

The other man went over the steps, slowly, his mind full of unspoken questions.

'Fine,' said Tim. 'You've got it. *Adios.*'

Tim Hara knew he was leaving Janet Lander with a man who could be trusted. He rode off, conscious that this was best for a lovely young girl and a man with too many harsh trails behind him.

Sure — he had left behind some puzzled people but maybe Luke Dugald would fill them in, and by that time many things might be clearer. If they were not, it would be because he was dead!

He rode through the changing country and after some hours saw the first signs of the encroaching desert lands. Then he saw the Yellow Hills again and began to think of what lay ahead. There was the unknown woman, prisoner for some reason that only Dane Lander knew. That alone was reason enough for pushing on. He had to find her, identify her, clear up the mystery for all time. That was his job and his pardon hung on it. He'd be Tim Hara, a free man, and the details on the wanted poster would be scrubbed out. But there was more to it. He had to break Lander.

In a way, Tim felt sympathy for the big autocrat. Lander was a loner like himself, a man whose past damned him. For Dane Lander there was no chance to scrub out his crimes. He would have to pay for them. The mystery of the woman in the cave would have to be revealed. Lander would lose his power, and maybe even the love of his daughter.

As Tim got close to the hills on his slow-moving horse, he saw a momentary flash of heliograph and grinned. Lander's spy system was working just fine!

He rode through the gullies, checking the lay of the land for possible future reference. He saw a man on a lookout rock and he waved to him. The man waved back.

Then he was entering the basin and the ride was over. He had his story ready for Lander. Sure, Janet was staying with the Hertzogs — that was all. Anything about the attempted lynching would lead to questions, and bad answers would induce suspicion. And there would be no mention of the man he'd had to kill.

Sure, Janet could tell her father many

little things, but with luck that would mean nothing. Much would happen before father and daughter met again.

After taking the roan to the livery, Tim had to report to Dane Lander. Tim tied the bandanna firmly around his neck before entering Lander's office. The big man sat behind his desk and kept Tim standing.

'I take it Janet is staying with the Hertzogs.'

'Yeah. They seemed happy to see her. The old galoot wanted me to stay on but I figured to ride back.'

'Then John Hertzog will see my daughter safely back here?' Gritty blue eyes surveyed Tim. 'You had no trouble on the way?'

'Trouble?'

'Wal, we do have Indians — and there are lawmen out Palermo way . . .'

'There wasn't any grief, Mr. Lander.'

'Good.' Dane Lander rose and smiled. He walked around his desk and went to a cupboard. He poured two glasses of neat whisky. 'Here You've done a good job.'

'It was pretty simple,' Tim said, accepting the drink.

Lander grinned. 'Good health.'

Tim drank and felt the liquid sting his tongue and the lining of his still-sore throat. He swallowed with difficulty.

When Lander dismissed Tim, the big man walked to a window and watched him walk to the bunkhouse. Suspicious by nature and trained by experience to notice little things, he wondered why Tim Hara had had difficulty swallowing a glass of spirits. And why was his bandanna so tight around his throat on such a hot day?

Nothing had happened on the ride, he'd been told. Of course, men lied about stupid little things — Lander was surrounded by liars and cheats — and there were times when he was sick to death of them all.

13

The Woman In The Cave

'When do we take him?' Dirk Schulman growled.

'Tomorrow,' Tim said.

'Why not tonight when we can get the drop on him? The other rannigans will be asleep. That's the best time — we'll just stick a hogleg in his back and tell him to take us to his gold and dinero cache.'

Tim Hara leaned on the pole corral. 'I said tomorrow, *amigo*. I've got plans.'

'Kinda cagey, ain't you? I want to know . . . ' Dirk Schulman flicked wary eyes at a passing man, then his gaze fastened on Tim. 'What've you been cookin' up, partner? Remember, I'm in on it. Double-crossin' wouldn't be healthy.'

Tim Hara stared right back. 'Hell,

Dirk, I need you. One man can't handle Lander and get his money at the same time!'

Dirk Schulman would have to be used, Tim thought, but there would be precious little wealth at the end of it for the fat renegade. He would be used and that was all.

'Tomorrow, eh?' Dirk muttered. 'You mean a daylight job? Why?'

'I need sleep for one thing. And tomorrow morning will be just right, my friend. I'll tell you more then. We can take Lander and settle any rannies who might figure to side with him. See you tomorrow — and button your lip!'

'You don't need to tell me that!'

'Fine. Just one more thing — send as many of these hellions ridin' out on the badlands as you can. Can you arrange that?'

'I'm Lander's *segundo*,' Schulman growled. 'They'll do as I say.'

'You know what we need. Get a party out on a wide loop trail to the west. Tell 'em to head for the Rio Grande. Tell 'em there's gold out there — a mule train — any damn thing. I leave it to you — but get 'em out of this camp after sunup. That gives us time.'

'And what's my story if Lander sees 'em headin' out?'

'You can spin the biggest lie of your life, *amigo*. Just make sure those galoots are hittin' dust as early as possible.'

That night, as he lay in his bunkhouse bed, enjoying the hard comfort of blanket and straw mattress, Tim Hara considered that the fat, treacherous Dirk Schulman had his uses. The man's greed would be his undoing. Somehow he knew Schulman would terminate his career at the end of a gun.

Tim Hara smoked a last cigarette and thought about Janet and the unknown woman. There were things in this assignment that he cursed. He cursed General Charlton and Captain Morgan for involving him. On the other hand, his fate would change for the better — or he could be snuffed out in a split second by a piece of accurate lead. Nothing was sure-fire, and tomorrow might see a day of errors.

He fell asleep. Darkness and silence was wrapped around the camp in the hills.

Then the sun clawed through a wide blue sky and men were roused from their slumbers. Tim opened his eyes and grinned warily as he saw Dirk Schulman prodding bad-tempered rannigans and rapping out orders. It was crazy that these men should take orders from a bullying fat man after they'd rejected discipline in the normal world.

Tim Hara went his own way. He wasn't sure if Lander was watching from his house. The movement of men and horses was carried out smoothly by Dirk Schulman and might not provoke any curiosity because there was always some activity inside the fort. Men slipped out singly or in twos.

Tim watched the men leave from one of the high lookout posts. He saw the shapes of men and horses bob occasionally into view in the gullies leading towards the desert. It seemed that Dirk had gotten events under way.

Tim chose the spot for the bonfire. He built the heap with dry twigs broken from scrub that littered the hill. There were plenty of dried mesquite roots. There was browned grass which would fire and smoulder and make a lot of smoke. Dried-up desert plant leaves were plentiful. He gathered them quickly, then he set flints around the pile of gunpowder which he had broken out of several rifle cartridges that morning. The flints were important. A striking rifle slug had to hit them. The gunpowder had to ignite — and then the bonfire. It was tricky, but a few well-placed shots would do it.

When he got back to the basin, he looked up. Sure, he could hit that bonfire from this angle with a Winchester.

He tramped back to the bunkhouse. The place was empty. He checked his

Colts. They were fine. He had more than enough slugs in the leather clips around his gunbelt.

He met Dirk Schulman outside the livery. A man was inside, attending to some horses.

Tim Hara walked away with the fat man. 'Everything all right?'

'Sure. I got that galoot fixin' some nags . . .'

Tim laughed grimly. He wanted only his roan. They wouldn't need pack animals. And maybe Schulman wouldn't need a horse.

'How many men left in this place?' Tim asked.

'I couldn't get rid of all of 'em. Must be about ten still kickin' around.'

'How many up in the lookouts?'

'Three.'

'Rifles?'

'Sure, they always got hardware.'

'Get them down. Tell Sam to cook up some extra grub for them. That always keeps a ranny busy.'

Tim Hara rolled another cigarette

and waited. He pushed his battered stetson back, smoked and watched the main house.

There was no sign of Lander. He might be reading; he had plenty of books in his study. He was a strange man. Again Tim Hara felt understanding for him. But sentiment was weakness in a land of lawlessness. Dane Lander's crimes made Tim's own recklessness seem small stuff. The outlaw had led men on many raids in the past, often four-day rides over a wide area, to rob and very often kill in the process. With Lander's law he had created his own hell.

Dirk Schulman hurried up, big boots digging the dusty earth. 'I got them galoots eatin' like it was fiesta time in the bunkhouse.'

'No lookouts?'

'Nary a one! First time for years. You figure they might start shootin' at us if they see us ride out with the loot?'

'We'll worry about that if the time comes.'

Tim Hara knew it was time to move in on Dane Lander. With every minute that passed the big man might appear and ask awkward questions.

'Let's go,' Tim muttered.

They walked boldly up to the main door of the house. So far their appearance and manner would excite no suspicion if they were being observed. They reached the veranda. Dirk Schulman turned the door handle and they entered the wide lobby. Mexican vases stood on a table; a skin rug lay at the threshold of a room; an Indian drawing hung on a nearby wall. Dirk Schulman picked up a little brass bell and rang it, the customary way to see the big boss. Sometimes Hoo Chung showed up to answer the summons, but on this occasion Dane Lander himself emerged from a room and strode towards them.

He wore a yellow shirt and dun pants, shining black leather boots. His gun hung low in the solitary holster. 'Yes, men, what is it?'

'I wanted to see you . . . ' began Tim Hara and, smiling, he moved easily to the big man.

'You've got something on your mind?'

The first part of it was easy. Tim Hara stepped to Lander's side and plucked the gun from the big man's holster. At the same time, his Colt jabbed into Lander's side. Seeing the play, Dirk Schulman hurriedly produced his own weapon and pointed it at the startled outlaw boss.

There was silence for a long time as the three men stared hard at each other.

Then: 'Schulman, you can't do this,' Dane Lander said.

'You've got the dinero!' Dirk Schulman rasped out. 'We want it. That's it.'

'You'd kill me — cross me — for money?' Dane Lander stared at the fat man with his terrible blue eyes.

'Why not? I've been workin' like a rat — and for what? Nothing! I've got nothing!'

'Put that gun down and I'll give you

a bonus,' said Lander coolly.

Tim Hara prodded with his gun. 'This play is for keeps, Lander. If Dirk decides to take your money, I'll kill you now — right where you stand. So don't try any more of that.' Tim changed his tone. 'Dirk, he'd trick you. You know that. You wouldn't leave this place alive — let alone with money or gold!'

'Yeah. Yeah, you're right.' Suddenly Dirk's fear of his boss, ingrained over the years, dropped away and he gloated. 'You've been treatin' me like dirt, but now we've got the drop.'

'How do you intend to get out of here alive?'

'We've got plans,' Tim Hara said.

'And how do you fit in, Hara? Who are you?'

'It's a long story, Lander,' Tim said, 'and I haven't got time to elaborate. Now get movin'. Back to the rear of this house . . . '

'To the gold,' said Dirk eagerly.

'To the caves, Lander,' Tim put in. 'I guess you've got keys to the doors back in those tunnels . . .'

'How do you know about the tunnels?'

'I know. Start walkin'.'

'You'll never get out of the Kingdom alive. I've got men who'll shoot you down.'

'Not if I threaten to kill you unless we're allowed to ride out. But we'll get to that later. Right now, Lander, I want to look into that cave at the end of a tunnel — the cave with the big wooden door, the place used as a prison for that woman.'

Dane Lander had turned under the initial threat but now he froze. 'You've been spyin'!'

'Move! We're wastin' time.'

'What do you know about the cave?'

'Just that you've got a prisoner. Now just move, damn you, Lander, or I'll kill you on the spot!'

The big man began to walk. He led them to the rear of the rambling house, opened a door and moved down a rocky tunnel. As they walked along the

201

natural passageway into the cliff, Tim Hara picked up a lantern which burned on a ledge.

'Why do you want to see the prisoner?' Lander asked.

'I've got good reasons.'

'Don't do this, Hara! You don't know the loathing — the terror — I've had to endure!'

'It's not my problem. Just go straight to that door and open it. I want to see that woman — and then you can explain.'

'Why? Why? Who are you, Hara? Who sent you here?'

'Push on, Lander. I'm here and I want answers — that's all you need to know.'

He had to force the man ahead. Lander stumbled. Prodded along by Tim Hara's gun, Lander reached the wooden door behind which Tim had heard the woman's moans. A gleam of light showed above and below the door.

'Open up, Lander!'

The outlaw leader brought out keys

from his pocket and turned his haggard face to Tim Hara. 'You're going to humiliate me, Hara. You know the truth, don't you?'

'Not quite. I have some information — and I can guess the rest — but I have to see this woman.' Tim hardened himself. 'I've seen a photograph that was taken many years ago. A good-lookin' woman, Lander. But I don't expect to see much resemblance now.'

'There is none! Oh, God, Hara, for years I've dreaded that there would be something like this — or that Janet would discover the secret! I should have killed the poor wretch — but again and again I found I couldn't!'

Suddenly the sound of wild laughter tore through the lantern-illuminated air. A sound of hammering hit their ears. The door shook as a hard object was banged against it.

'She's mad, Hara! Utterly mad. Leave her here to rot! Come back to the house and I'll tell you everything!'

'Open the blasted door, Lander!' Tim

gritted. 'I have a job to do and by hell I'll see it through to the end!'

Dirk Schulman had been puzzled for some time. Now he growled, 'What in thunder is this all about? Where's the gold, Lander? That's what I want. What's this about a woman?'

Tim Hara reflected grimly that Dirk's presence would be a nuisance when he realised there was no gold for his dirty hands. Then Lander spoke:

'You won't get any gold, Dirk. Hara isn't interested in gold.'

'What in tarnation is behind that door?' Dirk demanded. 'What's all that crazy laughin' and cryin'?'

'It's a woman,' said Tim Hara. 'I want to see her — try to identify her.'

'Listen, I aim to get the gold and money!' Dirk snarled. 'I ain't interested in anything else.'

'Later.'

'He's goin' to fool you, Dirk,' Lander said.

The fat man's nerves jagged him into swinging his gun at Tim. 'The blazes with what's behind that door unless it's gold!'

'No gold there,' said Lander.

'Holster that gun, Schulman — or point it elsewhere,' Tim grated.

Dirk Schulman began to sweat and his fear centred on Tim Hara. He felt he was being fooled. He was jumpy, uncertain.

'Damn you, Hara — who are you givin' orders to? I want to see that gold! I ain't sure about you — maybe you're fooling me. What's all this talk about a woman? Is that her — that mad yellin' and cryin'?'

'The gun, Dirk! Holster it!' Tim ordered.

The fat man's gun had been wavering, pointing at Tim and then Dane Lander and then back again. All at once Dirk Schulman roared an obscenity. His gun levelled, and Tim Hara knew he was going to trigger.

A Colt exploded in the tunnel and its slug hit hard into the heart of the fat man. Tim Hara had whipped his gun from Lander's ribs and fired.

Dirk Schulman, dead, sagged to the smooth rock floor.

'Open that door,' Tim Hara said. He felt cold, devoid of pity.

Dane Lander turned a key. The door swung slowly open.

A ragged, staring, hunched woman with the appearance of a mediaeval witch faced them momentarily and then turned and ran back into the cave, screeching insanely.

'Take a good look, Hara,' Dane Lander said. 'You want to know everything? All right — that's my wife, Laura. My wife! The wife of Dane Lander! She's been mad for years — stark, raving mad! I brought her here to the Kingdom in the very beginning. No one knew she was here except a man I paid to feed her — and he kept his trap shut on pain of death!'

'She's General Charlton's sister,' said Tim Hara. 'You ran off with her — disappeared for years. No one knew where you were living — or even if you had married her — '

'We were married, then Janet was born. When the madness began to appear in Laura we moved around a lot. As her spells of craziness got worse, I vowed never to let Charlton know about it — my pride, I guess. He hated me. I wasn't good enough for his sister. So I told people that she'd died. Janet went to live with a woman she knew as her aunt in Abilene. She wasn't really a relative — just a kindly woman; and she, too, kept her silence. I guess she was afraid of me.'

'You could have sought medical advice for your wife.' Tim watched the man.

A hard man, Dane Lander — but this secret was his weakness, like the soft underbelly of an animal.

'Don't you understand?' Lander's face contorted. 'That mad woman is my wife! The wife of Dane Lander! Even before I became an outlaw I was always respected — looked up to! Men feared me. At first I was able to hide Laura away when her — her craziness came on in a kind of a spasm. But it got worse. She tried to attack me more than once. About this time I heard of the Yellow Hills. I went out exploring. Laura was then hidden away in a lonely shack up in the San Antonio hills and Charlton thought she was dead. He didn't bother much, for all his damned pious remarks. I take it he sent you, Hara, to spy. But why? How did he guess?'

Tim said, 'A man came to Fort Worth with the story of a woman hidden away in a cave here. He was only half-believed, but General Charlton had to know. I got the job . . . '

'You, a wanted man?'

'Can any other kind get into this place?' Tim paused. 'Lander, you took a rotten situation and made it worse. You, the big man, couldn't take it. But you'll have to now. You're goin' back to Palermo. I've got a posse waitin'. It's all been planned — '

'Oh no, my friend!' Dane Lander

lunged into the dimly lighted cave.

Tim Hara levelled the gun and then hesitated.

It was a fateful delay. Tim couldn't understand his reluctance to kill this man. Maybe it was because he liked him in some strange way.

Then there was a terrible cry of agony from inside the cave. As Tim rushed forward, his Colt at the ready, silence descended.

He saw Dane Lander standing over a huddled figure, a heavy stool in his hand. Blood welled from the woman's head and made a pool on the cave floor.

'I've done what I should have done a long time ago.' Lander breathed. 'She's dead. She was beyond all help . . . '

'Turn around and get back to daylight, Lander,' Tim snapped. 'I feel sick.'

They went back along the tunnel, then through the house and into the sunlight. The brightness was such a contrast to the dim tunnel that Tim felt, for a moment, that he was suffering a nightmare.

But he knew it was all too real and that he had to hand Lander over to the law. One thing was certain: Janet would never learn about the horrible end of her mother. He'd see that General Charlton kept that story hushed. And for himself, he would not be seeing that lovely girl again.

She'd marry and maybe she'd be happy, leading a good life with a fine man. She'd be a credit to the Hertzog family. It was better that way. He was a loner — all the way.

Tim Hara, feeling the breath of real freedom against his face, went to ignite the bonfire on the hill; the signal to the invading posse.

Lander's Kingdom was finished.

THE END

A TOWN CALLED
TROUBLESOME

John Dyson

Matt Matthews had carved his ranch
out of the wild Wyoming frontier.
But he had his troubles. The big
blow of '86 was catastrophic, with
dead beeves littering the plains,
and the oncoming winter presaged
worse. On top of this, a gang of
desperadoes had moved into the
Snake River valley, killing, raping
and rustling. All Matt can do is to
take on the killers single-handed.
But will he escape the hail of lead?

THE WIND WAGON

Troy Howard

Sheriff Al Corning was as tough as they came and with his four seasoned deputies he kept the peace in Laramie — at least until the squatters came. To fend off starvation, the settlers took some cattle off the cowmen, including Jonas Lefler. A hard, unforgiving man, Lefler retaliated with lynchings. Things got worse when one of the squatters revealed he was a former Texas lawman — and no mean shooter. Could Sheriff Corning prevent further bloodshed?

CABEL

Paul K. McAfee

Josh Cabel returned home from the
Civil War to find his family all
murdered by rioting members of
Quantrill's band. The hunt for the
killers led Josh to Colorado City
where, after months of searching, he
finally settled down to work on a
ranch nearby. He saved the life of an
Indian, who led him to a cache of
weapons waiting for Sitting Bull's
attack on the Whites. His involve-
ment threw Cabel into grave danger.
When the final confrontation came,
who had the fastest — and deadlier
— draw?

RIVERBOAT

Alan C. Porter

When Rufus Blake died he was found to be carrying a gold bar from a Confederate gold shipment that had disappeared twenty years before. This inspires Wes Hardiman and Ben Travis to swap horse and trail for a riverboat, the *River Queen*, on the Mississippi, in an effort to find the missing gold. Cord Duval is set on destroying the *River Queen* and he has the power and the gunmen to do it. Guns blaze as Hardiman and Travis attempt to unravel the mystery and stay alive.

BLACK RIVER

Adam Wright

John Dyer has come to the insignifi-
cant little town of Black River to
destroy the last living reminder of
his dark past. He has come to kill.
Jack Hart is determined to stop him.
Only he knows the terrible truth that
has driven Dyer here, and he knows
that only he can beat Dyer in a
gunfight. Ex-lawman Brad Harris is
after Dyer too — to avenge his
family. The stage is set for madness,
death and vengeance.